LOCKDOWN PHANTOM #1

Compiled & Edited by

D. Kershaw | Maggie Pawsey | S.N. Graves

Also available and coming soon from Black Hare Press

DARK DRABBLES ANTHOLOGIES

WORLDS
ANGELS
MONSTERS
BEYOND
UNRAVEL

APOCALYPSE
LOVE
HATE
OCEANS
ANCIENTS

BHP WRITERS' GROUP SPECIAL EDITIONS

STORMING AREA 51
EERIE CHRISTMAS
BAD ROMANCE
TWENTY TWENTY

OTHER VOLUMES
DEEP SPACE
WHAT IF?
KEY TO THE KINGDOM
DEEP SEA
BEYOND THE REALM

Twitter: @BlackHarePress
Facebook: BlackHarePress
Website: www.BlackHarePress.com

Cover Design	Dawn Burdett	www.dmburdett.com
Formatting	Ben Thomas	www.blackharepress.com
Editing	D. Kershaw	www.blackharepress.com
	Maggie Pawsey	
	S.N. Graves	www.sngraves.com
Read Team	David Green	davidgreenwritercom.wordpress.com
	Jennifer Hatfield	jhatfieldauthor.wixsite.com/website
	Jodi Jensen	jodijensenwrites.wordpress.com
	Lyndsay Ellis-Holloway	authorlyndseyellisholloway.webador.co.uk
	Stacey Jaine McIntosh	www.staceyjainemcintosh.com

TABLE OF CONTENTS

THE TORTURED SOUL OF TAER GARCIA

By Kelly Matsuura

"Before you open the jar, close your eyes and take a deep breath. Consider

whether you truly want to open it. For if you do open it, beware. You will release a darkness that will desperately fight to take hold of you."

The words of the old witch, Buni, echoed around in Taer's head as he sat cross-legged in front of the grave, gripping the jar tightly with both hands. He closed his eyes, breathed in, and knew he would open it. He had no choice.

An unbearable pain had sent him to Buni's rundown shack in the jungle of Landao de Sur. He had entered her domain a broken man and had given her everything of value he owned in exchange for one last chance to see his wife again.

"When the jar is open, allow it a

moment to release the spell and find its way. When the scent lessens, it is time to recite the chant and call forth your lost spirit."

Taer opened the jar and squeezed his eyes shut as the burning scent of the herbs flooded his senses. He shouldn't have been surprised that a spell to call up ghosts smelled incredibly foul, but hey, he was a first timer. He began the chant after the smell was no longer overpowering.

Part of him had expected the spell to fail, to be a giant hoax and leave him feeling a fool, but after a short time the ground beneath him began to tremble, and the shadows deepened around him. He continued to chant, focused hard and not rushing the words. He kept his eyes open, watching for the moment when Casama would appear.

Wisps of grey and white smoke weaved their way out of the grass-covered plot and filled out into a recognisable human shape. The ghost looked around the cemetery, finally settling on his caller.

"Taer, is that you?" Casama asked, peering closer. "What in God's name have you done?"

Casama had only been dead for a few weeks. Taer hoped that his friend had truly been in Hell, suffering for every agonizing second that Taer had experienced in the four months since his wife, Halina, had been murdered.

"I didn't bring you back to chit-chat, Casama. I only want to know one thing."

Taer wished so hard that he could put his hands around Casama's throat, but there wasn't any real physical way to harm a ghost. The best Taer could do was yank him out of the spirit world and tether him to the spell he had bought from Buni, who had promised that the foul ingredients Casama would be locked in the jar with, would be equivalent to a thousand cuts by a blade.

Casama crossed his arms and frowned in that 'I'm a highly-intelligent-professor' manner he had. "I know you think I had something to do with Halina's death, but I assure you, the police were only fishing. They wanted me to implicate you."

Taer laughed at Casama's lies. "That's the story you're sticking with? Alright, you get one more chance. Where is Halina's body? Where did you dump her when she'd given you what you wanted?"

Casama shook his head. "I was your friend, damn it. You should have trusted me."

Taer wasn't backing down. "Not going be helpful? Okay then, in the stinky jar you go." He recited the trapping spell from the piece of paper on his lap and watched Casama struggle against the magic that swallowed him inside the ordinary, kitchen jar. "Let's try again tomorrow night." He screwed the lid on, then buried the jar in the earth by Casama's headstone. Finished for the evening, he picked up his things and followed the pathway back to his car. Casama was going to tell him where to find his wife, or so help him, Taer would bury the bastard in that jar of torture for the rest of eternity.

***

"Do not open the jar more than four, five times at most," Buni had warned. *"The spell will increase its power, but it will do so by feeding on your own soul."*

Casama's tolerance for pain was, unfortunately, stronger than Taer had anticipated. He couldn't blame the witch's spell though—the concoction grew darker and fouler every time Taer opened the jar. He opened it night after night, for two whole weeks, without getting the information from Casama that he needed.

Taer ignored Buni's warning. The

spell had cost him his life savings, and if Casama could be stubborn and hold out, so could Taer. Wasn't his soul already damned for using black magic?

"Come on, Casama. Surely you've had enough of this."

Casama did seem weakened, finally. He didn't have a physical form anymore, and he didn't bleed, but the smoke-like texture of his spirit form was denser, blacker. He didn't move as freely as before either—he was pulled out of the jar each time Taer released him, but Casama no longer wandered, testing the boundaries of the spell.

"You don't seem to be doing too well yourself, old friend," Casama replied, his voice a sharp reflection of the inner pain swirling in his vapours.

Taer didn't need to check a mirror to know how terrible his appearance was. He had stopped going into work days ago, after five small children passing his office building ran screaming down the street, shouting about zombies rising.

His skin was sallow and sagging, and he had lost weight despite eating more than usual. His hair, previously glossy and thick, was now thinning day by day. He had woken up completely grey after the first night in the cemetery, and while logic had told him to give up his quest, he didn't have anything strong enough in his life to motivate him to consider letting Casama go.

"All I want is Halina. I don't care

about anything else."

"What will you do if you find her?" Casama asked.

"None of your damn business," Taer snapped. God, he was so tired. He only opened the jar for a short time each night, but the seconds dragged, and he had to keep alert in case Casama tried to get free.

"I did some bad things in my life, Taer. But I didn't do them to hurt you. I hate seeing you like this."

Taer sat up, alert to Casama's softening tone. He was close, very close, to confessing.

"I have this magic jar, and the spell inside will kill us both, most likely," Taer admitted. "You, Casama, have the power to end this right. What do you say?" It was as close to begging Taer would go, but it seemed to do the trick.

"Okay, you win." Casama threw his hands up in an action reminiscent of his human life. "That day, Halina wanted to go on a picnic. We went to Lake Wood. There's a little beach on the west side, hard to find. She said she'd been there with you before."

Taer nodded, brushing away tears. "I know the place. She's...she's there?"

"Yes," Casama answered with no emotion. "We had a huge fight about...I don't honestly remember now. Anyway, I buried her under a small papaya tree. It's the only one near that spot."

"Thank you." Taer was too choked up to ask more questions. What did it matter how, or why? Now that he knew where she was, he was in a hurry to leave.

Taer stood up, still holding the jar.

"What happens to me now?" Casama asked.

"One second." Taer screwed the lid back on the jar without reciting the spell to put Casama back in with it. Looking straight into Casama's eyes, he released him. "Go back to the spirit world. Finish your journey."

With a rush of the wind and a howl of pain from Casama, the smoke was sucked back into the grave, and Taer was alone one more.

***

"If you do get your answers, and you go to the grave of your wife, take only her

favourite flowers with you," Buni had advised. *"The spell I gave you was made to raise a killer, someone who deserved the torture the jar would give. It was not made to give life to the dead whom we loved."*

The fishing spot was off the lake road he remembered from years ago. Halina's family had often gone there on summer weekends, but only for day trips as camping was forbidden.

He arrived at the lake a few hours still before dawn and found the papaya tree like Casama had said. Even though the ground showed no sign of disturbance, he was confident she was here. He felt something, or was it only his imagination?

A few minutes of digging proved that

Casama had told the truth. Taer found bones, some with dried tissue on them still, but it didn't bother him in the least. Looking at his own bare arm beside the remains made him swallow hard; he could see he wasn't so far from the same fate.

Satisfied it was Halina before him, he sat back on the grass beside her grave and opened the jar. He recited the summoning chant he had used to bring Casama back to Earth. He read the words with confidence but rushed a little in his excitement to see his wife again.

The ground trembled, and the leaves above rustled, announcing her presence. He watched her white spirit swirl and dance for him, finally filling out to the long-missed sight of his beloved Halina.

She, however, looked around, bewildered. "What is this? What am I doing here?"

"Halina, my love. I can't believe I found you." Taer broke into sobs, the kind that swells from a deep pain, long-stored within.

"Who…do I know you?" The apparition peered at him closely but shook her head. "Your voice is familiar, yet I can't place you."

Taer leaped to his feet. "Halina, it's me! Taer," he implored her to remember him.

"No!" Her hands went straight to her mouth in shock. "Oh, Taer. What did you do to yourself?" One hand reached out to stroke his cheek, but he couldn't feel her touch.

"I know I look…different," he began, "The magic has had an unfortunate effect on me. But still, I convinced Casama to tell me where you were, and now I'm here to be with you again."

Halina continued to stare at him. "I don't understand… I'm sorry. I can't stay here with you. It isn't allowed. Plus, this magic you have released, it's so so dark, Taer. You should have left this alone, moved on with your life." She looked at him with pity. Not love, he realised, she only felt bad for his suffering.

"I think I get it. You know that I know about your affair with Casama, and so you don't think I should forgive you." This had to be why she was distant. "Well, it doesn't matter to me. All I want is for us to be together and have another chance."

"That's impossible," Halina whispered. "Please, you must release me now and let me return. If you do, you may eventually recover your soul."

What Taer understood now, and had for some time, was that he had lost everything. His wife, his money, his house. All he had left was his blackened, tortured soul.

"It's alright, Halina. I have reached the end of my quest and found my treasure. I know what to do now."

Before she had a chance to stop him, he gulped down the murky stew within the jar. It was the most repulsive combination of ingredients anyone could concoct he was sure, but after smelling it daily for weeks, he could bear it.

"Taer, no!"

Magic kept her locked in place, unable to free either of them. Taer began chanting the trapping spell, reciting it perfectly by heart. He faltered for only a second as Halina's features blurred in the smoke and the wisps formed a trail right into his open mouth. He felt her spirit burn its way down into his stomach and even though it was such intense pain, it was her, and he cried tears of joy to be connected to his love once more.

When Halina was fully trapped inside him, and he was so weak he could no longer stand, he wandered to the water's edge and kicked his shoes off. Yes, this was the perfect place to die.

"Not long now, my darling," he whispered to Halina. Could she hear him? It didn't really matter. Their last remaining scraps of humanity and soul were tightly entwined. He lay down on the bank and held a hand in front of his face. The skin was so loose, he pulled at it with his fingers, and a chunk came free.

"Well, look at that," he chuckled. "I'm Dorian Grey." He closed his eyes, his last thoughts before dying were of Buni. She was a strange old woman, but she must have had a kind heart to give him the spell. She must have known the outcome and understood; it was what he truly wanted.

"Heartbreak can be the most

unbearable pain of all. Revenge won't heal it. Saying goodbye won't heal it, either. Darkness will block it out for a time, but darkness is not forever. When you cross to the next world, what then? Your pain may well travel with you. A broken soul could be your eternal fate."

First published in *Twisted Tales*, Gina Watson, 2018

ANNUAL BEACH DAY

By D.M. Burdett

I closed my eyes and lifted my face to the hot sun, letting the waves splash over me as I floated in the whitecaps. I loved beach days—the fun, the warmth, the freedom.

I heard Benny's voice over the gentle lapping, and I peered back at the beach, finding him next to an undefined shape in the sand.

"Mama! Look at my castle!"

Mum got up from the blanket, a wide grin on her face, and padded over to fawn over Benny's creation. She ruffled his blonde hair, and despite the cold water, a warmth spread through me; it was great to see her smiling after everything she'd been through this last year. She looked up then—as if she sensed I was watching her—and scanned the horizon. Her smile faded; I knew what she was thinking. My sunny mood plummeted.

I began a lazy breaststroke back towards them, the sea roaring in my ears.

Splashing over the surf, I crept up to Benny's turned back and whipped my head, pebble-dashing him with cold water. He squealed, turning quickly, and looked up at me darkly.

Mum was ferreting in the cool-box and called out without turning. "What's up, Benny?"

"He just got a cold shower." I laughed as I slumped down onto the sand next to her.

She peered over her shoulder as Benny started to cry.

"What's up, honey?" she asked, pulling a packet of cookies from the box.

"Uh," I groaned. "He's just sulking. It was only water." I lay on my back and draped an arm across my face.

Benny continued to cry, and Mum went over to comfort him.

I lifted my head slightly and squinted at them, my hand casting a shadow across my eyes. Mum had wrapped him in her arms and was crooning in his ear. "For goodness sake," I muttered, rolling my eyes. *It was just a bit of water!* But Benny stared back at me with wide, accusing eyes.

Mum led him back to the blanket, and he shuffled behind her, peering over her shoulder at me.

"Don't cry, Benny," Mum soothed.

"He's a wuss," I said, rolling onto my side and propping my head up on my hand. I stuck my tongue out at him, and he disappeared behind Mum's back.

"Do you want a cookie?" Mum asked.

Benny shook his head with a loud sob.

Mum sighed and I sat up. "You're ruining our family day out," I said, my lip curled.

"Oh, Josh. Come on, honey. Tell me what's wrong."

"It's Marty," Benny whispered. Mum flinched.

"Don't blame me," I said, exasperated. "It's not my fault Benny can't take a joke." I flopped back down onto the sand, but I knew our beach day was coming to an end.

"Marty?" Mum asked quietly, a tremble in her voice. "Marty's dead, sweetheart."

Benny shook his head. "He's here," he whispered, pointing to a puddle of sea water that was slowly dissipating; back to the ocean.

THE ROOM ON THE RIGHT

By Matthew M. Montelione

South Haven, New York.

December 1782.

Former British Private Nathaniel Underhill took a deep breath of the brisk winter air and sweetly kissed his wife's hand. In Mary's company, the chaos of the American Revolution seemed to flit away as they rode through the quiet of the gently falling snow in the forest. Slim rays of the westering sun bounced about the white ground. "Soon this accursed war will be over," Nathaniel said to Mary, kissing her hand. "Perhaps then, we can truly enjoy the stillness of the country." The mere musing of peacetime with his wife in their cosy Long Island home brought a smile to his face.

The conflict was almost over. General Cornwallis had surrendered Yorktown to the rebels in 1781, and British war morale was at an all-time low. Deep down, Nathaniel had had enough of the political strife that caused so much death and destruction to enemies of common blood. He often wondered why King George III chose to fight the colonists rather than consent to any of their demands. But regardless of what Nathaniel, a cooper's son, thought on the matter, Great Britain knew that their worst fears were being realised after a gruelling seven years of combat; the Patriots and their French friends would be the victors in this bloody civil war. Nathaniel had already come to terms with it.

"Is your father truly giving us the Middle Island farm?" Nathaniel asked, frowning. "He knows of what I've done."

Mary clenched his hand. "My father cares not about your desertion. He often jokes that he would have done the same thing, had he enlisted in the service of a mad, stubborn king."

Nathaniel laughed. It was not genuine; he still felt guilty for deserting the royal army. Still, it was comforting to know that after the war, the newlyweds had a place to settle down and call home. Until then, they had no choice but to keep their marriage a secret and keep Nathaniel hidden from prowling royals and Patriots alike who labelled deserters as cowards and killed them. "I will take your word," Nathaniel said, forcing his mind away from his anxious thoughts.

The wind blew faster through the

snowy trees as they rode on through the pine forest. Nathaniel nudged his dark brown horse closer to hers.

"Archer is getting brazen," Mary laughed. "Show him how to behave, Nyx."

Nyx neighed in joyous approval of the frolic, her head pushing against Archer's.

Almost in an instant, winds ripped more ferociously, carrying heavy snow. Mary brought her steed to a halt, prompting Nathaniel to do the same. She pulled her coat tightly around herself. "The snow grows thicker by the minute, and it is getting late," Mary said, shivering.

Nathaniel took off his coat and wrapped it around her. "Shall we head back?"

Mary nodded in approval. "Yes, let us

return to our warm hearth."

"Right away, my love," Nathaniel replied.

They started on their way back. The snow fell harder. They had not travelled far when they came upon an unfamiliar spot in the woods. The couple stared into the bright sky, trying to locate the setting sun. But the snow continued its onslaught, obscuring the narrow trails they usually trod. Their eyes hurt as they squinted at the white sky.

Nathaniel raised his hands in anger at the heavens and muttered curses.

Their horses were almost up to their knees in snow and could see no better in white-out conditions than their masters.

Still, the Underhills continued,

spurring their beasts on through the violent storm. Crisp wisps of air bit through their coats; the winds howled more fiercely than before. Swaths of big snowflakes whirled past them. At the moment of despair, they noticed a splendid manor house before them as if out of thin air. They caught a glimpse of a roaring fireplace through one of the windows. Breathing great sighs of relief, they led their horses to a nearby shed.

The sight of the opulent residence was a saving grace to the cold travellers. Nathaniel tightly gripped Mary by her waist as they came to the front door. The door was black as night. Shivering and wet, Nathaniel grabbed the iron knocker and slammed it with immediacy. There was no answer. The only sound they heard was the raging winds.

"Knock again!" Mary said, her soft lips chattering.

Just as Nathaniel was about to strike again, the door creaked open.

A tall and solemn African house slave stood opposite the travellers. His candle illuminated his deep grey eyes, which pierced through them like arrows. The man's finely tailored clothes suggested that he was held in high regard by the owners of the house. He stared at them for what seemed like minutes.

"What business do you have here?" the glaring man asked.

"As you can see, a vile storm is rampaging outside. My wife and I seek shelter from the storm. I fear our lives depend on it! In the morning we shall leave and return with generous payment for your master, for his troubles."

The door warden stared at the shivering travellers before he spoke again. "Doctor Wickham is not home. But I suppose he would not want to turn away cold travellers. Enter. There is a fire lit in the sitting room." He stepped aside, allowing them to pass into the dark house.

The Underhills suddenly flinched. Why did the house, which at first sight brought feelings of salvation, now feel like a queer place amidst the inner darkness? The couple looked at each other for a moment, but overcame their anxieties and entered the home. Nathaniel brushed the snow off Mary and continued to hold her close. It felt good to be out of the snowstorm's wrath.

"Please, make yourselves comfortable," the servant said, ushering them into the spacious sitting room. "My name is Brutus, and if I may be of service, just ring the bell." Brutus pointed to a small, silver bell that rested on a nearby table.

Before Brutus could leave the room, Nathaniel stopped him. "Have you anything for us to eat? We are famished and have not supped."

"My apologies. There is no sustenance that can be spared at this time. Dr Wickham is not at home; he oversees such matters. However, I will bring some wine." Before the couple could convey their discontent with his answer, Brutus turned and walked away down a dark hall.

Nathaniel grunted and turned to Mary. "No food? We shall leave posthaste in the morning, as long as the snow slows."

Mary gave him a worried look.

It was all a very unfortunate result of what was a joyous frolic in the woods. They looked around the lavish room. A red chair rested near the fire.

"At least there is warmth here," Nathaniel noted, looking at a portrait of a richly dressed gentleman on a large estate.

"I suppose that's Dr Wickham," Mary said, following his gaze.

Suddenly Nathaniel spotted a goblet of wine on the end table near the chair. Brutus had not returned since he left them. "He could not have brought that so quickly," he said to Mary.

She looked with concern at Nathaniel, paying no attention to the mysterious cup.

He took her by the arm and pointed to the drink. "Dear wife, look! That was not there a moment ago! Who brought it hither?" A bout of dizziness overcame him. He staggered towards the chair.

Mary caught him, ushering him into the chair. She grabbed his hands and pressed them together under hers. "My love," she said, startled, "your hands are as cold as ice. You must rest here!"

Her urgency startled Nathaniel, and he tried to get up.

Mary insisted that he sit back down.

She went behind him and ran her slim fingers through his long, dark hair for a few minutes. Her gentle touch lulled Nathaniel to sleep.

The former soldier awoke to an empty room. His heart dropped when he realised that Mary was not there. He was deathly frigid; the fireplace had died down to embers. He grew woozy and let out an anguished shout. "Mary! Mary, my love!" he screamed. "Where are you?" Nathaniel yelled as he made his way towards the front door. He screamed until his throat was hoarse. Nathaniel tried to open the door, but it would not budge.

Brutus appeared from the hallway behind him. "She left, sir. Worry not; she left of her own accord."

Nathaniel turned to Brutus, red with rage and confusion. "Worry not? Tell me where my wife is!"

Brutus stared calmly at Nathaniel. The Englishman was about to throw Brutus down and pummel him, when the tall man finally spoke. "As I said, sir. She left of her own accord."

Nathaniel did not know what to think or what to believe. Had Mary left him in this dreary place all by himself? Was this some cruel joke she was playing on him for some God-awful reason? Was she outside in the storm, in need of aid? Or was she still in the house? Surely she would not leave him alone! He had to find her. Nathaniel wailed and pulled the front door with all his might. Still, it did not move. Were its hinges frozen? If Mary had left that way, it was hours ago. How long was he sleeping? He cursed and slammed his fists against the door in anger. The snowstorm raged on in the pitch-black night.

Nathaniel turned to engage Brutus. "How could she have left if—" he stopped himself. The house slave was no longer there. Nathaniel paused. In that moment, a thought so simple crossed his mind, he could not believe he did not think of it sooner. "The windows!" he shouted. All he saw through the panes was snow, but he had to try to break the glass and escape. He ran over to the fireplace and grabbed the end table. He hurled it at the window, expecting the glass to shatter. But it did not break. Over and over again, he tossed the table against the window until he grew weakened. Still, it did not shatter. He quickly tried other windows but found the same results.

His heart dropped again, and he felt more trapped than ever. He needed to find Mary. Just as he turned to ascend the staircase to the second floor, unexpected sounds of music flooded down from the upstairs and filled the house.

"What folly is this?" he exclaimed as he ran up the staircase. The clamour grew louder as he ascended. When he reached the upstairs hallway, it was dark, but he could make out the entranceways to two rooms on opposite sides at the end of the hall. The music grew louder. It was coming from the room on the left. Nathaniel was familiar with the instruments he could hear; angry trills of violas and violins and pounding thuds of a double bass. Cellos and a harpsichord wailed in dissonant tones. The composition was unlike anything he had ever heard before. It reminded him of Handel, but it lacked all the grace and humanity. *The shadow of Handel, perhaps. There is something sinister about this music,* he thought.

It was even colder upstairs than it was below. Nathaniel shivered, making his way to the room on the left and peering into the long, narrow space. He squinted to sharpen his vision against what seemed like fog. *It cannot be fog, you dolt! You are inside.* But all of his reason left him when he saw what was within the space. It brought fear to his heart beyond his wildest dreams.

Many candles, suspended in the air, drenched the room in a pale orange light. No wax dripped from the candles, yet they fiercely burned. The pallid musicians at the far end of the space vigorously played their instruments. Nathaniel looked around the room full of people. He gasped. These were not people at all. Their eyes dimly glowed in black eye sockets and their expressions were wanting. A few sat in chairs, staring ahead at the wall. Others were moving about with no apparent purpose, while others wailed in agony or threw themselves on the ground and convulsed, as if they were tortured by some unseen force. How they screamed! The mix of hellish sounds pierced Nathaniel's ears. Others stood and gawked at a most miserable sight near the musicians. Nathaniel wished his eyes had not followed their gaze.

A hideous mockery of nature danced in a most vile fashion to the clangs of the pale orchestra. The monster looked somewhat like a man, but in many ways, it seemed entirely inhuman. It looked more like an animated corpse with tattered pieces of decayed flesh dangling as it moved. Its odious mouth was sewn shut with thick black thread, stitches ran up and down its limbs. It danced and jerked as if a puppet master controlled it, yet there was no puppeteer. This demon had agency of its own. It let out an anguished scream, severing the stitches that held its mouth together.

Nathaniel could take the madness no longer. He yelled and fell to his knees.

At that very moment, the music stopped. The disgusting creature ceased its dancing. All the ghouls stared at him with hollow eyes.

He lifted his head and saw his miserable situation. His blood ran cold at the sight of it all; he felt frozen. He wished that he was home, warm and safe with Mary. *Mary!* He had to find her, no matter what devilish devices stood in his way. Vigour returned to his bones, and he sprang up, ready to fight the evil before him to the very end with his bare hands.

All at once, in hellish unison, the beings let out a blood-curdling wail. The monster reared its head back, stretching his long, gnarly arms to its sides as it shouted in horrific tones. The ghouls slowly advanced towards Nathaniel from all over the room.

Nathaniel braced himself and debated his next move.

Brutus appeared from out of the shadows. At this point, the servant's sullen face was an almost welcoming sight. Nathaniel did not trust Brutus, but he realized that he, at least, was not revolting, unlike the other terrifying spectres before him. Perhaps Brutus could help him escape this domain of damnation.

"You'll find no hope in this room, sir. None at all," Brutus said.

Suddenly the advancing creatures burst into flames. All of them afire! They did not fall but continued their advance.

Nathaniel stood in silent horror, his mouth agape. He stared at the abomination and its horde of ghouls, moving slowly but intently towards him.

"You may want to try the room on the right," Brutus whispered to him.

"The room on the right!" Nathaniel exclaimed. He had forgotten all about the other room. "Perhaps there is a window there that I could escape from!"

Brutus smiled and disappeared into the darkness of the hall.

With all the strength left in him, Nathaniel turned from the room of atrocities and ran across the hall to the room on the right. He swung the door open. Freezing high winds ripped through the house, blowing snow into the hallway.

The monster and ghouls wailed. They advanced closer to Nathaniel by the second.

Nathaniel felt as if he was caught between the fires of Hell and the arresting cold of death. Neither option appealed to him, but both rapidly closed in on him. He looked in the room on the right. To his shock, there was no actual space beyond the doorway. Rather, there was a roughly ten-foot drop to the ground, and beyond that, a snowy forest.

He did not try to make sense of the strange exit. *My way out!* he naturally thought, but he all too quickly realised the folly of his optimism. At the bottom, he spotted a rectangular, freshly dug ditch, carved into the earth despite the falling snow. He squinted and cried out. At the far side of the hole stood a tombstone. Nathaniel did not need to read the chiselled name on the slate to know that it was his.

Gathering his courage, he turned to his enemies. He raised his fists against them and yelled, "Come, foul works of the Antichrist! Come! Do with me as you will!" Just as he was about to charge at his stalkers, he found that he could not move. His body was suddenly cold and inanimate.

The ghouls relented, but the gangling monster inched closer and closer to him.

Powerless, Nathaniel watched in terror as the animated corpse approached him and stared at him with dead white eyes. Just as the creature, in flames, came upon him,

Nathaniel felt long fingers grip his heart and tug. He could do nothing as he fell backwards. With a firm thud, Nathaniel's motionless body fell into the ditch. All went black.

"Husband, can you hear me?"

Nathaniel awoke to the comforting sound of Mary's voice. He smiled, opening his eyes as her soft fingers grazed his face.

"Nathaniel!" she exclaimed, "you made it, my love! I feared you were lost to me. Thank God, and thank you too, Doctor Muirson! My Nathaniel is awake!" Her smile was ear to ear.

Nathaniel felt warmth return to his bones. A fire roared near him. He slowly looked around at a familiar sight. He was home! Mary sat beside him, and Dr

Muirson, a close friend of her father, sat in a chair near the fire. Nathaniel sat up in joy, hugging and kissing his dear wife.

"I feared I lost you, too... I had the most hellish nightmare! It felt so real. We went astray in a snowstorm, and came upon the house of Dr Wickham. Only, we found no welcome there. Before I knew it, I was trapped...alone in Wickham's dark prison, where a deplorable monster and its ghouls chased me into my own grave. I cannot recount to you the hideousness of it all." Nathaniel choked on his words and started to tear up. "I could not find you, my dear. I feared you were dead." The harsh, vivid memories of the house flooded back to his brain.

Mary's face went pale. "Did you

say…Dr Wickham?"

"Yes, the house we came upon in my nightmare was Dr Wickham's. I do not recall exactly what—"

Mary put her finger to his lips. "Hush, dear husband, and listen. I am afraid you are confused. Part of what you described was no dream. We did get lost in a snowstorm, and we did come upon the remains of Dr Wickham's home…but we did not know it was his, not at the time. Much of the house was burned to the ground, remember? Upon finding it, the bitter cold gripped you, my dear, and you fell. It was unexpected, and I was scared. I placed you on a charred chair, concealed inside the ruins. The power of the storm waned, and I rode to Dr Muirson's house with haste. I came back for you as fast as I could." Mary sighed. "I hated leaving you there. That decaying woodpile was deplorable! But it kept you out of the snow's wrath, at least. I knew I had to get you help, and I could think of no other way. I am so sorry, Nathaniel!"

Nathaniel was confused. If the snowstorm was real, was it all real? All those unspeakable terrors? "If it was not a dream, and you saw the house, then you know it was not burned at all! This is madness! Brutus answered the door and let us in. Enough games, Mary. You were there with me! Has your mind gone out to pasture?"

Mary looked at Nathaniel with tears in her eyes. "Oh, Nathaniel," she said as she pulled him close, "I will do whatever it takes to get you through this! I promise. Rest now, husband. You must rest."

Nathaniel looked at her strangely. "Get through what? I am healed, am I not?"

Dr Muirson's face was grim. "What your wife says is true, Mr Underhill," he said. "We found you amidst those charred remains, where she left you. If we had been any later, I know not if I could have saved you. By God's will, we were able to reach you in time."

Nathaniel huffed and tried to make sense of his predicament. "Well, who is Dr Wickham?"

Mary stroked Nathaniel's hands. "You tell him, Dr Muirson," she said.

Dr Muirson sighed. "I knew George

Wickham well. Or at least I thought I did. He was a great man of medicine, but he was not a kind man. When he was angered, he took to mutilating his slaves by stitching their fingers together, or their toes, or stretching their eyes apart. He committed many evils against those poor souls. After I discovered his barbarism, I planned on reporting his behaviour to the town officials. But our Lord had other plans. One night, while Wickham entertained many guests, his slaves and their native allies revolted and stormed the house. According to a servant girl, the intruders slaughtered the revellers in nasty ways, but saved the foulest death of all for the doctor. They stitched his mouth shut and then stitched him all over his body. Not a limb was spared. He must have died most slowly and painfully. Then, with the dead and dying within, they set the house ablaze. Many burned to ashes on that cold winter's night in 1758."

Nathaniel let out an anguished cry.

THE LAST TRAIN HOME

By Dale Parnell

It was with a heavier heart than I would have liked that I put my shoulder to the door and pushed my way into the pub, struggling to squeeze the oversized rucksack through the narrow doorframe. The warm, jovial air rushed up to greet me, carrying with it the noisy chatter from the fifty or so people that had crowded into this tiny backstreet pub on Christmas Eve.

It had been a tradition for a number of years now that on Christmas Eve a group of us from school would meet up at The Montague Arms in Norwich, so that we might catch up and toast the season. I would have usually arrived in Norwich a few days earlier, staying every year as I did at my parents' house, but this year the university had requested that I re-write some of my lectures in time for the new semester. Taking the opportunity for undisturbed work that this past week had afforded me, I had stayed at my little flat in Durham until the last possible moment before catching the train home. I had booked the latest train I could that would still allow me to make a stop at the pub and had promised my parents that I would be quiet when I finally arrived at their door.

The yearly tradition of meeting up with my oldest friends would usually have me in high spirits, but truthfully, I could not shake the dark mood that had been with me for the entire journey, and as old friends are liable to do, they soon noticed and commented that I was not my typical self, and they insisted that I tell them what was troubling me. When fresh drinks had been ordered, I took a deep breath and told the tale of events that had brought me home this evening.

***

Having locked up my flat in Durham, I took a taxi to a small, local railway station that lies twenty minutes away, Waldon Park. I would usually catch the train at the main station, but this year there was extensive renovation work going on, and I had been advised it would be easier to meet the train further down the line. When the taxi pulled into the carpark, I noted that the place looked deserted and was slightly frustrated as I had hoped to find a small café open where I could get a cup of strong tea and something to eat. I paid the taxi driver, and he pulled away, leaving me alone in the still half-light that is so typical of a late winter afternoon. Hefting the rucksack over one shoulder, I walked the short distance to the main entrance and into the small but perfectly charming foyer.

The floor was tiled in a mosaic of black and red diamonds, and the walls had been clad in rich oak planks, stained a dark chestnut brown by decades of varnish. My shoes squeaked on the floor, breaking the otherwise total silence that filled the space. Directly ahead of me was an ornate archway, the gates standing open and leading the way to the platform, only visible for a few feet before dissolving into darkness. The lighting looked pre-war and cast a soft yellow hue over everything, the filaments in the oversized bulbs clearly visible and burning white hot.

It was only after I had taken all of this

in that I saw her. On the right-hand side of the foyer were displayed the typical timetables and maps that you find in every rail station, and then on the left stood an old-fashioned ticket booth, constructed from the same stained oak and seemingly picked straight out of a children's book. And there behind the curved glass partition, was a lone figure. She appeared to be in her mid-twenties, not much younger than me, and as I looked around I saw that she was staring at me, and on her face was a look of such abject sadness that I was certain I felt my heart stop for a moment, like it was remembering the loss of a loved one. Her eyes were red and puffy and easily recognisable as belonging to someone who had been recently crying. I like to consider myself a compassionate person, and I confess I felt instantly moved by this poor woman and wondered what could have possibly happened to make her feel so sad on Christmas Eve. We held each other's gaze for a brief moment before she looked away, roughly wiping a sleeve across her face as if to scrub away the sadness. I stepped over to the booth, and slipping my rucksack onto the floor, I informed her that I had ordered a return ticket to Norwich. She tapped wordlessly on the keyboard for a moment, and after confirming my name and address, my tickets were printed and handed over.

"Thank you," I offered as warmly as I could, trying to keep any sign of pity out of my smile. "And happy Christmas."

This last phrase seemed to re-open whatever wound was affecting her, and she tried and failed to suppress a helpless sob before turning her chair away from me. I felt instantly embarrassed and guilty, and started searching the small space again as if I would find another member of staff previously invisible who would be able to help the poor woman. On checking the small black and green departure screen, I saw that I had around thirty minutes before my train was due to arrive.

"Is there anything I can do?" I asked, feeling completely useless. She didn't answer, tiny sobs still shaking her shoulders, and again I searched the foyer, looking for any clue or distraction that might help. Then, over by the entrance to the platform, I spotted the small sign directing the way to the tearoom.

"Is the café open?" I asked. "Maybe I can get you a cup of tea or something?"

This at least seemed to reach her, and she looked up, tears running down her cheek. She then shook her head and, speaking almost too quietly to be heard, said, "No, sorry, it's closed tonight."

I let out a sigh, offering a cup of tea was the limit of my abilities when it came to comforting anybody, especially a stranger. I was desperately trying to think of something else to suggest when the woman spoke again, although this time it was too quiet to hear.

"Sorry?" I asked.

"I have the key though," repeated the

woman.

***

Ten minutes later we were at a small table in the tearoom. The woman, who had introduced herself as Alice, had drawn the blind on the ticket booth and led the way round to the tearoom. The single bulb in the room blinked on after flickering for a few moments, and Alice busied herself with making a large pot of tea, finding and wiping clean two mugs. After sorting through endless cupboards, she eventually found a basket of those small sterilised milk pots, and after loading a tray she joined me at the table. The noise of the water boiler had made any conversation pointless, and so now we sat opposite each other in a sudden silence, Alice fidgeting in her seat slightly.

I took a small sip of tea, the scalding water burning my lip as my brain raced, desperate for some topic of conversation that might take the edge off the situation.

"Have you been here long?" I asked.

"Yes, a long time," replied Alice, directing her comment to the tabletop. Eventually, she looked up briefly and brushed the loose hair away from her face.

"I'm sorry about this," she said.

"Don't be," I replied. "Christmas can be a tough time for people."

Alice was staring down at her lap, and I wasn't sure she wanted to talk after all, when she began to softly speak.

"It's always hard being here. But it's worse at Christmas. I just…I get so lonely."

"I suppose these small stations don't get used much anymore," I offered, trying to be understanding, although I'm not sure if she was actually listening to me now.

"There used to be lots of people, but they've all gone away. I want to leave, I really do, but I'm afraid."

"It can be scary, leaving a job and starting over. But if you're not happy, then maybe it would be for the best?"

She looked up suddenly, her eyes staring straight into mine and her hands had shot out across the table and were now grasping mine.

"You could stay, couldn't you? Just for Christmas. You don't have to stay forever, but just for Christmas."

I felt my cheeks flush pink, and I

pulled my hands back awkwardly.

"Look, Alice. I'm sorry, but…"

"No, you have to go," she interrupted, her voice cracking, her body slipping back to its former self, quiet and still.

We sat in silence and finished our tea, the only sound the rhythmic tick coming from the large clock face above the door to the platform. I wanted to say something, anything, that would make things better, and stealing a glance, I could see newly formed tears running slowly down Alice's cheek. I reached a hand across the table for hers, but she pulled them back, letting them drop down into her lap.

"Your train is coming," she said, not looking up.

A glance at my watch told me it was

due, and gradually the far-off rumble of a train forced me to my feet. I gathered my coat and rucksack, pausing at the side of the table.

"Alice, I..."

"Go," she whispered.

Unsure of what else to do, I left, the small brass bell above the tearoom door resounding down the empty platform.

***

The train pulled out of the station, and I had been in my seat for around ten minutes when the conductor appeared at my side. I had been unable to shake the image of Alice's face as I left her sitting in the tearoom, and the conductor had to cough a few times to get my attention.

"Tickets please," he asked again.

"Sorry," I replied. My coat was on the seat beside me, and I routed around in the pocket for my tickets. Finding them empty, I checked my wallet, thinking I may have transferred them there. When that proved fruitless, I checked the smaller pockets on my rucksack. Now I was stood up and re-checking every pocket again, the conductor looking on disinterestedly.

"I had them," I offered, starting to panic that I had left them behind. "I picked them up at the last station."

"Which station?" asked the conductor, as I continued to turn my pockets out.

"Waldon Park," I replied, throwing my coat down into the seat opposite me and searching around underneath the seats and down the aisle of the train.

"Waldon Park is closed, sir. If you don't have a ticket, you will be required to purchase one."

This stopped me dead.

"No," I replied petulantly. "I picked up my tickets at the booth in Waldon Park, where I just got on the train ten minutes ago.

"You may have boarded the train at Waldon Park, sir, but the ticket office has been closed for years. Now where are you travelling to?"

"Don't be stupid," I said, getting agitated. "I was there less than half an hour ago, the ticket seller is a woman named Alice, and she printed my tickets. I had a cup of tea with her!"

"Sir, I'll ask you to keep calm, please.

Now if you don't have a ticket, you will have to purchase one, or you'll be asked to leave the train at the next stop."

We argued around the point for a further five minutes until I eventually showed the conductor my booking reference, and he agreed to print a new set of tickets for me. For the remainder of the journey, the conductor gave me a wide berth, and I was grateful to him for it. I was furious at what I assumed was his incompetence and fully intended to make a complaint when I got to Norwich Station.

***

"What happened?" asked Mike, his glass hovering in front of his face mid sip.

"I spoke to the customer service desk at Norwich, and they said the same thing.

Waldon Park station has been closed for twelve years. The lady at the information desk said she thought there had been a fire, but she couldn't remember."

"Come off it!" replied Mike, trying his best to force a laugh, although it seemed to lack any genuine humour.

I couldn't think of anything to say, the best I could manage was a shrug of my shoulders, and we all finished our drinks in silence. Eventually, Daniel, always the most practical of us all, clapped his hands together, making us all jump, and declared that it was his round. As he made his way around the table to the bar, he leaned a hand on my shoulder, and I felt the briefest of squeezes. Gradually the bar felt warmer, the Christmas lights around the windows seemed brighter, and when Daniel returned with drinks, the conversation returned to its usual good humour.

When the bell rang for last orders, I hurried to the bar and ordered a round of whiskeys, to better protect us all against the cold of the long walk home. I didn't tell any of the others, but I ordered an extra one and left it behind on the bar. Maybe one day Alice will be ready to leave, and when she does, she can join us for a Christmas drink.

First published in *Bramble and Other Stories*, 2019

STAY WITH ME

By Cindar Harrell

The house was just as I remembered it.
And that's what scares me...

I had never been there before, never stepped foot inside the woods surrounding it, and yet I knew exactly what it would look like. The crumbling front porch had the ivy wrapped around the sides; the windows were shuttered up except for one at the top, an eerie glow coming from inside.

I had never seen pictures of it. I just knew.

Something wanted me to come here...but why?

I hugged my arms tightly around my chest, rubbing them to try to get warm. The sun was setting and the chill was sinking in, although part of me didn't think it had anything to do with the oncoming night at all.

Carefully, I walked up the stairs to the door. The doorknob was rusted; I could barely turn it at all. It held fast.

Locked? Who would bother locking this dump?

Walking back down from the porch, I tried to peer around the corner of the house. It was even darker back there, nothing but dense forest shrouding it.

Taking a deep breath, I went ahead. The back of the house looked to be in even worse condition, part of it falling off, scattering debris on the ground.

The back door was equally rusted, but the door was so rotted that the wood might have given way with enough force. Before I could try, however, a sound from behind me drew my attention.

What was that? I scanned the woods but didn't see anything at first. Suddenly, a faint light appeared, a shining beacon in a world of darkness. Without hesitation, I went into the forest, chasing the mysterious light.

As I walked further into the woods, the light moved. It would vanish without warning, leaving me alone in the darkness, but then pop up somewhere else. A different direction.

Where are you leading me?

As I went deeper, the light appeared less often and was dimmer. Eventually, I made it to a small clearing with an old well in the centre.

What is this doing way out here?

I looked over the stone edge to see if there was anything inside.

The light couldn't have been coming from here. Could it?

Something shimmered at the bottom, catching my eye. Is that water? I guess it's not dried up after all. It did it again, but brighter. Squinting, I leaned over the edge further, straining to see.

What is that?

Something hit my back hard. I screamed, falling into the darkness. It seemed like I fell forever, like I would always be falling.

Is this what Alice felt like? I wondered, tears streaming freely from my eyes. I reached back behind me, clawing at the stone sides, ripping my nails off. When I finally hit the bottom, pain exploded throughout my head and body. The air was forced from my lungs, and I struggled, wide-eyed, to breathe. I gasped, clawing at my throat, begging my lungs to work again.

Closing my eyes, I tried to calm down and steady my heartbeat.

Just breathe, just breathe.

Slowly, the air returned, and only the numbing pain was left. I looked up. The moon was perfectly silhouetted by the ring of the well's opening. If the circumstances were different, it would have been beautiful. *What happened? It was like I was pushed, but I was alone in the woods, wasn't I?*

A sound like laughter echoed through the cramped space.

"Who's there?" I asked the darkness.

The giggling came again. "It's so nice of you to come and visit me," the voice of a little girl said. I peered into the shadows, trying to see her.

It's too tight in here for anyone else.

"Where are you?" I asked.

"Does it matter?" she giggled once again.

I winced as I tried to move my leg. Pain shot through it and I knew something was broken. "Yes, it matters!" I shouted. "I need help! Can you help me?"

"Help you?" Even though I couldn't see her in the darkness, an image appeared in my mind of a little girl tilting her head to the side in wide-eyed confusion. Where did that picture come from?

"Yes, help. I'm injured and I need to get out of here."

"But why would I want to help you leave?" she asked.

"What?" I tried to move again, but the pain ricocheted throughout my body stemming from my leg.

"You came to visit me! Why would I want to help you leave?"

"Are you saying you live in that house?" I said disbelievingly. There was no way anyone still lived there; it was completely uninhabitable.

"I used to, but not anymore."

Her words weren't making any sense to me. I could feel the panic rising in my chest, edged with encroaching desperation.

"Look, that doesn't matter. I will come back if you help me get to a hospital."

"What's a hospital?"

Children and their damn games!

"Quit playing around! I need a

doctor!"

"A doctor? One used to come around when my mom got sick, but I haven't seen him in a long time."

"What are you talking about? There are no home doctors around here anymore."

"You're weird." She giggled again.

I opened my eyes from their clenched positions and saw the face I had envisioned earlier. She was standing in front of me, wearing a pale blue dress, her hair tied in twin braids. She had her hands behind her back and a large smile on her face.

"What?" My eyes widened as I stared at her. "How did you get down here?"

"Same way as you, of course!" She pointed up to the opening of the well. "Like

I said, no one has come to visit me in so long. It can get very lonely down here."

"How long have you been down here?"

How is she not injured? Surely her parents are missing her...

A look of concentration crossed her face. "I don't know. It's hard to keep track now."

"Have you been here since yesterday? Was it light outside when you fell in?"

She nodded.

She's been down here for hours!

"You aren't hurt are you? You don't look injured."

"I used to be! When I fell it hurt very badly, and I could hardly move. My legs didn't work, but now they are fine! See?"

She did a little dance and twirled, and I once again wondered how there was room. I looked at her legs more closely and my blood ran cold. She wasn't standing, not really. She was floating. It looked like she was floating just above my own mangled legs. That made me look closer at her. I leaned up on my elbows as best I could. Her dress was dated, and she wore a little apron that looked like it had flour on it.

"So... Do you know what year it is?" I asked, trying not to panic at the thought that I was trapped in a well with a ghost.

She thought a bit more. "Hmm...I don't know, I never really paid much attention when I went to school. I much prefer to stay home and help my mom bake in the shop."

"Stay home? They let you do that?"

"Yeah! A lot of the kids stay home to help their parents! Many of the boys stay to help work in the fields." She paused for a moment, then looked up. "I really am glad it worked though."

"What worked?"

"My sign! I sent you a message so that you would come visit me! Of course, I didn't know it would be you specifically, but someone."

"You are the one that led me here?"

"Of course!" she said excitedly.

"Well, don't you think it would be nice if we could... play outside of the well? I mean, it's so cramped in here that I don't think there is much we can do."

The little girl looked up, thinking. "That's true! But when I tried to get out before, it didn't go well... Daddy didn't like it."

"Daddy? What do you mean he didn't like it?"

"Well, even though it hurt really bad, I tried to climb up." she pointed to the opening. "I would have made it too! But then Daddy stopped me. He probably just thought it was too dangerous for me to be climbing. And he was right! I fell down again."

"What did he say?" My heart was racing. Did her father really kill her? She didn't seem like she knew, but from what she was saying, it certainly sounded that way.

"He screamed 'no' really loudly. He grabbed my arm, but then I fell. But if you have to get out, you can try!" she said with a happy little bounce.

I don't know if I can make it with my leg like this. I looked up again. Everything was dark, just the moonlight illuminating the area. *But I'll die if I do nothing.*

I nodded to the girl and struggled to stand on my good leg. Clenching my teeth to try to brace for the pain, I reached up and clutched the rocky walls. I cried out as I raised my leg and closed my eyes.

Come on... It may hurt, but it's better than dying down here!

"That's it! You can do it!" I heard the girl call out from below.

I tried not to think, just to keep pushing

myself on, going up and up.

"You're almost there! Just a bit more!"

I tuned her out, not wanting to give myself false hope. I just needed to keep going. Finally, my hand wrapped around the edge of the well.

Yes! I looked up, but a dark shadow was blocking the moonlight. Something grabbed my wrist.

"You shouldn't have answered my daughter's call. Now you will join her." a deep man's voice said.

"No..." I whispered, desperately trying to hang on, but he was too strong. He forced my hand from the wall and shoved me back. Once again, I found myself falling into the abyss. I landed with a loud crack as my skull collided with the bottom.

There was nothing but pain and darkness.

"Daddy really does think of everything! Now you can stay and be my friend forever!"

THE WAIT

By Amber M. Simpson

I wander these rows of final rest with nothing to do now but miss you, this ache of longing a small death all its own.

I run my fingertips along the hard, etched letters of your name, wishing for the warmth of your flesh instead of the chill of your stone. How unfair it is that it should still be smooth to the right of your birthdate, while my own date of death has been carved for six months.

We bought these plots side by side so we could lie together.

Now all I can do is wait for you.

First published in *TheDrabble*, 2019

HER NEW SISTER

By Wondra Vanian

The elegant Victorian on the edge of Rapid Falls, with its faux towers and wraparound porch, was the perfect place for Patsy and her seven-year-old daughter, Amanda, to start a new chapter in their lives. That was the official line, anyway. In truth, it was both within Patsy's paltry budget and as far from her ex-husband as was humanly possible to be without leaving the continental US.

Patsy counted herself lucky that her daughter was so young. Moving was just one big adventure to Amanda. She had no lifelong friends to leave behind and was years from hormone-driven, angst-ridden sulks. Hopefully.

Moving was difficult enough, without any of that. Finding time to pack, research properties, call lawyers, and enrol Amanda in a new school district took up every moment of Patsy's already limited free time. As if any single mother had such a thing.

Single mother.

God. Would she ever get used to that?

Technically, the divorce hadn't gone through yet, but Patsy and Franklin had been separated for over a year already. She didn't need a twelve-thousand-dollar piece of paper to tell her what she already knew. Patsy's life as a married woman was over. No sense dwelling on it; just put on the proverbial big girl panties and deal with it.

Or, move across the country to avoid dealing with it. Also a valid option.

Frank hadn't done a thing to stop the move. Whether he was eager to keep the peace or just to avoid any ugly scenes between his ex-wife and his new twenty-two-year-old girlfriend, Patsy couldn't say. She wasn't sure that she even cared.

Okay, she *did* care—but she knew she shouldn't.

The thing Pasty had really worried about was how Amanda would take it. But, as it happened, her amazingly adaptable daughter handled the situation brilliantly. Amanda made games of packing up all their belongings and insisted on picking the songs for their "forever road trip." During one Skype date with her grandparents, who had retired to Florida many years before the girl was born, Amanda confided that she was excited to have a bigger room to decorate.

"And," she said, bouncing in place, "it has *lots* of rooms. So, if Mommy ever finds a new Daddy, there's plenty of space for sisters. Not like this silly old house…"

Patsy, who had been packing books in the background, had been forced to grab the bookshelf for support. A new Daddy? Heaven forbid!

Amanda was right about the space, though. In addition to the master bedroom, the one Amanda had already claimed as her own, and the one destined to become a home office, the old Victorian had two more bedrooms than they really needed.

Plenty of space for sisters.

Maybe. One day—when Patsy got over the sight of her soon-to-be ex-husband under a rail-thin, blonde co-ed… When she learned to believe a man when he said he was "working late." When an innocent smile from a hunky bartender didn't send her defences slamming shut faster than you could say, "Gin and tonic, please."

Probably not.

But at least there would be plenty of room for family if and when they made the trek to BFN, Michigan for a visit. There would be room for Patsy's married-forty-years-and-counting parents, her just-celebrated-their-tenth-anniversary brother, and her younger, still-a-newly-wed sister. Plenty of room in those wounds for a few good handfuls of salt…

Stop it, Patsy ordered herself. She'd promised herself she would save any breakdowns until after they were all unpacked and settled in their new home. They hadn't even finished packing yet.

***

"Mommy, it's *huge!*" Amanda

exclaimed, jumping up and down on the spot.

"It sure is, kiddo," Patsy agreed. It was even bigger than it looked in the photos the realtor had sent. Something about that nagged at Patsy.

She must have looked at more than a hundred properties, across several states. Most of them had been smaller than the one Patsy and her daughter were leaving behind. The ones that weren't needed a *lot* of TLC. The one they stared up at needed a paint job but was twice as large as any of those. As they climbed the creaking wooden steps to the front door, Patsy found herself worrying that the old house might have structural problems the photos hadn't conveyed.

What have I gotten us into? she thought as she slid the key into the lock.

Patsy caught Amanda's hand before the youngster could take off at a run. "Let's go together, okay?" she said, eyeing the large foyer warily.

"Aww, Mommy!"

Amanda was obviously eager to see her new room. She tugged at Patsy's hand to hurry her along when she stopped to test the strength of the boards under their feet.

"It'll still be there in five minutes," Patsy promised her daughter. *I hope.*

Patsy's fears were unfounded. The floorboards were sturdy, and the bedroom door didn't fall off its hinge when she pushed it open. In fact, Patsy couldn't find a single thing to fault with the house, bar a rather large spider web under the kitchen sink. A thorough and cautious exploration of their new house revealed that it was in surprisingly good condition, considering its age. Considering the *very* low price she had paid for it.

Surprisingly, she told herself, *not* suspiciously. There was absolutely no reason to call the realtor and demand to know why such an amazing house had come so cheap. None, whatsoever. Good things could happen, Patsy told herself, despite what her recently failed marriage had taught her. It was difficult to resist the voice of doom whispering in her ear, telling her it was too good to be true; that the roof would probably fall on them as they slept; that the house had been built on swampland

and would sink into the ground in the very near future.

But none of those things happened. The worst thing that happened was a disagreement between mother and daughter over whether the cheerful, yellow walls in the downstairs bathroom really needed to be coated with the leftover glitter gloss from Amanda's freshly painted room (they did not). Amanda even spent the whole night in her new bed—something Patsy tried not to get too emotional about.

Patsy had to admit, after two days in the house, that she had worried herself sick over nothing. The house was… well, perfect. Once she allowed herself to believe it wasn't too good to be true, Patsy found she liked it almost as much as Amanda did.

And, if Patsy sometimes wondered what family life would have been like in the gorgeous old house had her husband not abandoned them, she kept that hidden deep away, where her daughter would never see it. It was remarkable how well the little girl had taken to her new home. If anything, Amanda seemed happier there than she had been before the separation.

Very often, when Patsy walked past her daughter's room, she would be greeted by the sound of childish laughter as she played made up games with her dolls. The behaviour was a little unusual for the girl—the dolls had been in storage for a couple of years—but Patsy was so happy to see her daughter happy that she didn't think too much of it.

At first.

***

Patsy was on the way to her office when the sound of an intense conversation brought her up short outside Amanda's half-closed door.

"That's not funny," she heard Amanda say. It was scary how much her daughter sounded like a mini version of herself. Then things got *really* scary.

"It is so!"

That was most certainly *not* her daughter's voice.

Patsy burst into the room without stopping to think. Her brain was stuffed to bursting with thoughts of every horrible news report she'd ever seen about children.

"Hi, Mommy!" Amanda said happily,

hopping to her feet. The little girl was totally unfazed by her mother's sudden appearance.

Gaze sweeping wildly around the room, Pasty didn't immediately answer. She went to the closet and threw it open, shoving clothes aside to peer into the darkest corners. When she found nothing, Pasty dropped to her knees beside the bed. Nothing.

She looked in every corner of the room, even the spaces that were too small to hide a person. *Someone* had to be there—but how? Patsy had changed every lock the day they'd moved in, just like her father had warned her to. And she'd taught Amanda stranger danger, hadn't she?

"Mommy? What's wrong?"

Patsy could barely hear the question over the pounding of her own heart. Instinct made her wrap her arms around Amanda protectively, pulling her close.

The girl laughed. She snuggled into the embrace. "You're silly, Mommy,"

When Patsy was able to convince her brain that Amanda was safe, she forced her arms to release the little girl. Amanda dropped a kiss on her cheek, then bounded off to grab a doll. Patsy watched her play in silence for a minute before asking the question that burned on her tongue.

"Honey?"

"Mhm."

"Who were you talking to?"

The little girl froze, fingers tightening around the doll she held. Her eyes went to an empty spot nearby, then back again. "No one," she lied.

Amanda wasn't the type of child to fib, which was why they were so easy to spot when they slipped past her lips.

Patsy beckoned her daughter forward. "You won't be in trouble," she promised, "but I need you to tell me the truth, okay? Who were you talking to?"

Amanda chewed that over for a minute. Her eyes darted back to the spot she'd been playing. She nodded at the empty space there.

"Trinity," she said finally. A smile tugged at the corners of her lips.

"Trinity?" Patsy asked, equal parts confused and concerned. "Who's that?"

"My new sister!"

The excited exclamation had two effects. It reassured Patsy that her daughter hadn't let some stranger into her room and simultaneously squeezed her heart so hard she thought it would stop beating. How could Patsy explain to her sweet, hopeful daughter that she wouldn't have a new sister for a very long time?

If ever.

Better to just let her have what was obviously an invisible friend. Amanda had never had one before, but she'd never been completely uprooted before either. Just a normal, healthy reaction to an incredible life change. Nothing to worry about. Patsy could have cried in relief.

"Okay, honey," Patsy said, giving her daughter a smile. She racked her brain, trying to remember what the parenting books had said about invisible friends and came up with nothing. Oh, well. What harm could it do? "Okay," she said, "You girls have fun."

Amanda beamed and returned to her dolls.

If she thought that would be the end of it, Patsy soon found she was wrong. Dead wrong.

***

It started with near misses, the kinds of things that were easy to dismiss. A handful of marbles scattered across the hallway. A stovetop left on when no one had been cooking. A roller skate left halfway down the stairs. When Patsy stepped out of the shower onto the jagged shards of a broken glass jar that had no business being in the bathroom in the first place, she decided she could no longer pretend they were just accidents.

"Amanda Elizabeth Stevens!"

Patsy found Amanda in her bedroom, having a whispered conversation with thin air.

"Young lady, I've been calling you."

Amanda looked up, saw Patsy wrapped in a towel, hobbling on one foot, and went back to her strange conversation.

"You need to stop!" she hissed at nothing.

The invisible friend thing was cute when it started, but it was getting old. These days, Amanda spent more time talking to Trinity than she did anyone else.

She barely even said hello to her grandparents when they Skyped.

"Young lady, I'm talking to you!" Patsy snapped impatiently. Her foot throbbed.

"Look what you did!" Amanda said to the empty space in front of her.

When Amanda continued to ignore her, Patsy caught the girl by one arm and led her down the hall to the bathroom. She pointed at the broken glass. It was stained with her blood. "What do you call this?" she demanded.

Amanda looked at her feet, refusing to answer.

"You could have hurt me!" Patsy said.

The girl finally looked up. She wore a belligerent look, though her eyes swam with tears.

"I didn't do anything!" she insisted. "It was Trinity!"

Patsy closed her eyes on a sigh. Kneeling in front of the girl, she said, "Honey, I know you wanted to have a sister, but Trinity isn't real."

"She is! She—"

"She isn't. You have to trust Mommy, okay?"

Amanda looked ready to argue but Patsy held up a hand to silence her. "Try this for me," she said. "Just ignore her. Pretend Trinity isn't there. Stop talking to her. If you do that," Patsy told her daughter, "she'll go away."

Then, Amanda sniffed loudly, and all Patsy could do was sweep the girl into her arms and hold her until she stopped crying.

"I don't know, Mom," Patsy said later that night. "I mean, I thought Amanda handled the move so well but now…"

The face on the other end of the internet was full of patient understanding. "I'm sure it's just a misunderstanding," Patsy's mother said. "I remember a time when you were little, and I was certain you were trying to kill me." Laughing, the older woman continued, "I convinced myself that you'd the cut the straps of my sandals."

Patsy thought back. "Is that when you broke your arm?"

Her mother nodded.

"Mom," Patsy said. "I was at summer camp when that happened."

More laughter. "I know! That was the

only way your father was able to assure me that I'd bought a crappy pair of shoes and my dear, sweet little girl wasn't trying to murder me."

Patsy could have argued that moving a broken jar from the kitchen to the bathroom seemed pretty deliberate but knew it wouldn't do any good. Her mother adored Amanda and would never conceive of the girl doing anything wrong—exactly the way a good grandparent should be.

***

After the incident in the bathroom, Amanda changed, becoming withdrawn and sulky. She kept her promise and stopped talking to her imaginary friend— but she had also stopped talking to Patsy, her classmates, and her teachers. Patsy tried to give her daughter time to work through…whatever was bothering her. Until she walked into Amanda's room and found the girl huddled under a blanket, sobbing into a pillow.

"Mommy?" the little girl said in a small voice. "I don't want a sister anymore. She's mean."

Patsy's heart broke. She sat on the edge of the bed and started to pull Amanda into her lap, stopping when the girl winced.

"Honey? Are you okay?"

Amanda nodded, but her eyes were glued on the corner by the door. Patsy found herself glancing in that direction without realising it. Of course, there was nothing there, but Amanda's gaze was so intense it was easy to believe there would be a mean little girl staring back at her.

Patsy shivered. She pushed back the unicorn covered blanket and froze. Angry purple bruises covered her daughter's arms.

"Did you do this?" she asked, horrified.

Amanda shook her head.

"Did someone else?"

The girl nodded. Patsy's concern turned to fury.

"Who?" she demanded. "Who hurt you, honey?"

Patsy was in full-blown Mama Bear Mode and, when she found out who had dared touch her daughter, she would…

"Trinity."

Her anger fizzled away. Patsy couldn't

fight something she couldn't see. She needed help.

***

Dr Herbert ran a practice less than twenty miles away. Amanda's teacher recommended the man's services, saying that he'd help with other "difficult students." Though Patsy bristled at the suggestion that her daughter was "difficult," she had Amanda booked for an appointment the next day. Those bruises, scattered across the girl's arms, scared the life out of her.

"It isn't unusual for children to go through these phases after an upheaval," the doctor assured Patsy. "Their behaviour can become extremely erratic as they struggle to cope with feelings they don't understand."

Patsy frowned. The way she saw it, there were two explanations for the bruises: either Amanda had hurt herself and was lying about it or someone else had hurt her and she was lying about it. She didn't have a PhD in child psychology, though, and was paying the man two hundred dollars an hour, so she'd give him a chance. Whether she could do that while keeping the disbelief from her voice was yet to be seen.

"She was fine after the move," she argued. "Happy, even."

The doctor nodded as he scribbled a note on the file in front of him. "Stress can be deferred," he said without further explanation. "Maybe now would be a good time for Amanda and me to have a little talk," he suggested, dismissing Patsy entirely.

Amanda sat on a beanbag amid an array of toys in a corner of the room, staring into space. She hadn't touched any of the toys. Dr Herbert rose to join the girl, asking Patsy to wait in the lobby. Reluctantly, she obeyed.

Their "little talk" seemed to take an age. Patsy flipped through every magazine in the lobby at least twice and checked her phone, oh, about a million times. The receptionist occasionally glanced up from the sleazy romance novel she was pretending not to read behind her desk. Eventually, after Patsy had started working her way through the stack of children's books on the table, the doctor's door opened. He ushered Amanda out and asked Patsy to join him.

"Well," he told Patsy, "Amanda has herself quite the invisible friend, doesn't she?"

Patsy nodded, growing more frustrated by the minute. She'd already explained about Trinity! Had the man been listening at all?

"Completely normal," he assured her as he scribbled on his pad. "Most children have an invisible friend or two at that age. That's not what concerns me."

Oh, really? The invisible friend is somehow less concerning than the physical wounds?

Patsy had to bite her lip to keep from exploding at the oblivious doctor.

"The thing that causes concern," he said, "is the animosity exhibited by this invisible friend. This…" he shuffled his notes, looking for the name.

"Trinity," Patsy supplied. Again.

"Ah, yes, Trinity." The doctor stopped. A strange look crossed his face.

Patsy grew uneasy. "Is there a problem?"

Dr Herbert shook his head. "No, no. It's just… That name seems familiar…"

Unease grew into fear. "Doctor?"

"Well," he said, giving himself a hard shake. "Never mind all that. Let's focus on what's behind your daughter's 'friend,' shall we?"

Dr Herbert, it seemed, was confident that the bruises were a form of self-harm, which didn't make Patsy feel better at all. Self-harm? Her baby? She was only seven! It took the rest of their insanely expensive hour to assure Patsy that everything would be okay. At the end, he hurriedly advised Patsy on the best way to help her daughter overcome the funk she'd gotten herself into and the best way to deal with Trinity, then sent them on their way with a promise to see them again next week. The car ride was painfully quiet, but Patsy refused to give up.

"Did you like Dr Herbert?" she asked.

Amanda just shrugged.

Patsy tried again. "Did you introduce him to Trinity?"

The girl shook her head.

"Why not?"

Mulling over her answer for a moment, Amanda eventually said, "Trinity doesn't like him."

"What about me?" Patsy said, afraid she already knew the answer. "Does Trinity like me?"

Amanda stared out the window and refused to answer. A chill that had nothing to do with the open window ran down Patsy's spine.

***

The doctor's advice didn't seem to do much good. They were due to meet him again in three days and nothing had changed. Amanda was every bit as withdrawn and uncommunicative as she had been before the appointment. Patsy would never give up, but it was starting to feel like a lost cause.

"I don't know, Mom," Patsy said, rubbing her aching eyes, "maybe I should get a second opinion…"

Her mother's concerned face stared back from the computer screen. "Never mind all that," she said. "Why don't you two come stay with us for a few weeks? I'm sure a change of scenery will do wonders." The old woman had never had much respect for what she called "shrinks." According to her, there was nothing that couldn't be solved by more sun and less work.

Easy for her to say; her kids were raised. Patsy sighed.

It wasn't the first time Patsy's mother had suggested a visit. Hell, she'd started not-so-subtly dropping hints that they had plenty of room the moment Frank moved out. At first, Patsy had been against the idea. She was a strong modern woman. She didn't have to go running to Mommy and Daddy the moment things went wrong. Now?

It doesn't have to be forever, she told herself. Like her mother said, just a couple of weeks. A change of scenery. What could it hurt?

"You know what, Mom? That sounds like a great idea. I'll book the flights now."

Patsy packed her bag the next morning while Amanda slept, feeling more and more confident she'd made the right decision. Tired and anxious, she needed a break as much as her daughter. They would…

Her hand stilled on the case's zipper. Was that…laughter?

It had been so long since she'd heard her daughter laugh that Patsy didn't immediately recognise the sound. She stopped and listened. There it was again.

Leaving the case on the foot of the bed, Patsy followed the sound of laughter. She pushed open the door to Amanda's bedroom but found it empty. Strange, she hadn't heard the girl rise.

The phone in her pocket buzzed as she poked her head into the kitchen. Empty. Patsy answered the call while straining to listen for the laughter that had suddenly gone silent. "Hello?"

"Ah, Mrs Stevens," the caller said.

"*Ms.*," she corrected automatically, moving through the house.

The caller coughed awkwardly. "My apologies, Ms. Stevens. It's Dr Herbert."

Patsy paused her perusal of an empty spare room to stare at the phone. "Dr Herbert?"

"That's right."

"Is something wrong?" she asked, moving on to the next room.

"Oh, no," he said quickly. "No, nothing like that. It's just that I remembered where I'd heard the name Trinity before, and I thought you might be interested."

"Though," he continued in a conspiratorial tone, "mostly I was proud of myself for remembering and wanted to show off a little." The doctor chuckled. "You know what it's like."

"Mhm."

There! The laughter came again as she made her way down the hallway. It was louder at the end.

"Anyway," the doctor said. "My predecessor, Dr Benjamin, once told me the story of a young boy with an invisible friend. Her name was Trinity. Sad, sad story," he added.

The laughter had to be coming from the attic. There was nowhere else to go. Patsy's delight at hearing laughter fill the large house quickly faded into annoyance. She'd told Amanda never to go in the attic by herself. The large window that overlooked the backyard didn't have any sort of latch on it to stop a curious young girl from opening it and climbing out onto a terrace that looked none too steady.

"Hmm?" Pasty was too distracted to care much about what the doctor was saying.

"Sad," he said again. "He claimed his invisible friend told him to do things. Said this Trinity hated his parents and wanted them gone."

"Wait. What?" Another child with a malicious invisible friend who was also called Trinity. What were the chances?

"What happened?" she asked.

Sad, sad story.

"Why is it a sad story?" Annoyance was quickly replaced by fear. A chill spread across her flesh, making the small hairs on her neck rise.

Dr Herbert *tsk*ed and said, "Well, the parents had unfortunate accidents. The mother took a tumble down the stairs, if I remember, and the father… I don't remember, exactly, but he died a few weeks later."

"That's terrible," Patsy said, horrified.

"Indeed," the doctor replied. "It was before my time but I'm sure the public library will…"

"What happened to the boy?" Patsy interrupted. If she had been worried about Amanda before, she was fucking terrified now.

"Well now, I only have local gossip to rely on and we both know how unreliable that is," Dr Herbert answered, oblivious to the fear in her voice, "but I think he eventually returned home. Became something of a hermit. Yes?"

The conversation became muffled. It took Patsy a moment to realise he was talking to someone in the room with him. He cleared his throat when he returned. "According to my assistant," the doctor told Patsy, "the gentleman in question passed away years ago, at a considerable age. I'm not normally the type to gossip," Dr Herbert assured her, "but given our conversation on…"

She'd stopped listening.

Things clicked into place so rapidly, they left Patsy reeling. Why the house was so cheap. All the little accidents. The bruises. It all made sense.

Except, of course, that it didn't make sense because it couldn't be *real*.

Trinity wasn't an invisible friend. She was a ghost.

Alarm bells sounded in Patsy's mind. The phone fell from her hand as she rushed up the stairs. Patsy was in such a hurry that she didn't bother watching where she was going. At the top of the stairs, she tripped over something and fell. Hard. Her forehead slammed against the wooden floor. She saw stars. When her vision cleared, Patsy pushed herself up, looking around to see what she had tripped over.

There, at the top of the stairs, was a bundle of clothes and hair. It looked like a doll. A large doll. Wearing Amanda's dress. A trickle of blood ran down the doll's throat, seeping into the floorboards.

"No!"

Please, God, no. It can't be. Not my baby girl...

She started to crawl toward the body, but the sound of a child's laughter stopped her in her tracks. Horrified, Patsy turned to find herself face-to-face with the thing she told her daughter couldn't be real.

"Trinity."

***

Thanks to a call from a concerned doctor, Officers Blackmore and Logan were already on their way to the elegant Victorian on the edge of Rapid Falls. Unfortunately, they were just minutes too late to stop Patsy Stevens from throwing herself from the large window that overlooked the backyard and an hour too late to stop her from slitting her daughter's throat.

It was a sad situation, they agreed, but not all that surprising. Rumour had it the woman's husband had traded her in for a younger model, and that kind of thing was bound to drive someone a little crazy. Officers Blackmore and Logan stood back and took notes while forensics did their thing in the spacious attic.

"Your turn to inform the family," Blackmore told the other man.

His partner groaned. "Not this one," he complained. "I'll do your paperwork for a week if you do it."

Blackmore considered the offer.

Before he could answer, Logan held up a hand and peered through the open door.

"Did you hear that?" he asked after a moment.

Raising an eyebrow, Blackmore asked, "What?"

The other man shrugged. "Nothing, I guess. Thought I heard a kid crying…"

GRAVE REVENGE

By Matthew M. Montelione

Under an autumn moon I met the ghost of Arabella Floyd. She was the wife of Richard Floyd IV, my chief subject of historical study. Richard IV was a wealthy Loyalist, an American colonist who sided with Great Britain in the American Revolution. When the Patriots won the war in 1783, he had no choice but to leave his Long Island home, banished under pain of death. For some reason, Arabella did not leave with her husband; she died from unknown causes in May 1785. Although their family had lived on the island for generations, their memory was snuffed out by the victors. Later, sometime in the 1900s, what remained of the Floyd house burnt to the ground. Arson was suspected, but never confirmed.

It was no coincidence that Arabella appeared to me on my nightly walk: I had studied her and her family for months; I felt close to her, like I already knew her. The setting was perfect, the bright moonlight added a certain clarity to all around me; crisp air blew fallen leaves over the roads and across the lawns of suburban Mastic. As I passed the old gated cemetery which housed Arabella's remains, I saw her pale ghost atop her weathered limestone grave. Her sunken eyes stared at me, and I stared back, frozen in my tracks. I felt horror, as any person would, at seeing a spectre for the first time, but I faced my fears.

I analysed her pallid yet beautiful form. She was dressed in the finest colonial attire, and for a moment, her beauty rendered it hard for me to believe that she had been dead for over two hundred years. Something about her otherworldly glance swayed me to her will; I was strangely attracted to her wispy form.

At length, she spoke softly: *Help me. Avenge me.*

Her words pierced through my heart. "How?" was all I mustered.

"Bring me the charred page. You know of what I speak. Avenge my family." With that, she vanished into thin air.

My heart raced. "The charred page," I said. I knew exactly what she was talking about! During my research, I came across a burned page in the Floyd family bible at the preserved house and archives of William Floyd, Richard IV's Patriot cousin and neighbour who signed the Declaration of Independence and did nothing to help his Loyalist cousin after the war. William's grand estate became a federally-protected museum after his descendants donated it in the twentieth century. There, William's items and documents were carefully preserved, including the eighteenth-century bible. Arabella wanted me to steal the burned page. Possessed with the drive to satisfy her, I started planning my sacrilegious heist.

Morally speaking, I didn't want to steal the page. After all, I was a historian. The act was altogether immoral, illegal, and against everything I stood for as a preserver of the past. But Arabella was counting on me. Failing her seemed like a greater guilt than tearing out the page of a historical bible that was rarely opened anyway. The next day, I made an appointment with the archivist, Jeanine, to return to the collection.

Finally, the day arrived. My heart was pounding as I entered the old house; I pondered if Jeanine could hear it as she placed the Floyd family bible before me. She hovered around me as I carefully turned old pages. If I was going to swipe the desired page, she had to go.

"Jeanine," I coyly asked. "Can I take you up on your past offer to see that nineteenth-century Civil War uniform?"

"Of course, Michael," she said, smiling and opening the wooden door that led to the storage room. She shut the door behind her, not sensing my ultimate betrayal.

I found the chosen page and looked it over. The burn marks trailed along the fringes of the old parchment. I thought it strange that this page was the only one that was burnt. I cringed and wrestled with my conscience as I carefully ripped it out, coughing loudly to cover the sounds of tearing parchment. I quickly folded the page and stuffed it into my pocket just in the nick of time; moments later Jeanine emerged from the storage room with the dusty uniform. I pretended to be incredibly interested, even though in reality I couldn't care less about it. Finally, she broke off our discourse.

"Well, it's five o'clock," she said sorrowfully. "Time to close up. If you'd like to work with the material again, come back soon and make an earlier appointment."

"Sure, no problem," I said as I snapped

a few cellphone photos of random bible pages and the uniform.

"Do keep me posted on your manuscript!" she added.

"Will do," I said with a sly smile. "Thanks again!" I got into my car and left, feeling both accomplished and guilty.

Under the cover of nightfall, I brought the page to the cemetery. My eyes widened and delighted as Arabella's feminine form appeared over her tombstone.

"I have it!" I exclaimed, taking the folded page out of my pocket. "The page you seek!"

Arabella smirked, and in the blink of an eye, she stood about a foot away from me, behind the gate.

I stared at her deep blue eyes in

absolute wonder, studying every detail of her figure: her heart-shaped face and dainty ears, her dark hair tied back in a bonnet, her slender form sculpted by her dress. I hoped that my efforts had pleased her.

At length she spoke. "Only I can reveal the secrets of the page," she said. "But I am dead and cannot grasp it. You must read it to me."

I held the burnt page up to the light of the moon. "It's hard to read such tiny print in this light," I said.

Arabella laughed; an otherworldly chuckle that I hadn't heard before. "Look *closer*."

Suddenly, an illuminated script appeared in the margins of the page.

"Read it to me," she said, seductively,

"and my family will be avenged. *I* will be avenged."

I squinted, doing my best to read the passage. It was in Latin; I had no idea what it meant, or if I was correctly pronouncing the words.

"Mortui...ultionem...sequitur...inglori a."

Icy fingers gripped my heart. I felt numb. I could do nothing but helplessly stare as the ghost of Arabella usurped my body.

Arabella Floyd breathed deeply the cold, crisp air of autumn. She walked to the house of William Floyd and burned it to the ground.

BLOOD ROSES

By Ximena Escobar

Leaf by leaf, the forest undressed.

Twig by twig, the bird nests collapsed.

Feather by feather, hair by hair, little bodies stripped, twitching bare on the ground like agonised worms, slowly absorbed into the soil.

Hoot by hoot, howl by howl, the woods silenced, bark peeling off the tree trunks till nothing was left of the forest but bone.

Nail by nail, tooth by tooth pierced the ground—skin and flesh also shedding—all hunters' prey themselves too, to the dark earth's resolve, and bait for those who would come seeking them.

Those who didn't, the forest came for them.

Silence turned to song, it reached them in their deepest sleep. Oscillating into their skulls, its haunting whistle stopped their hearts that they could better listen to its wilful beat; hear it, fear it, before they burst and evaporated into the air—travelling as mist into the woods where bare trees waited like receiving hands, drinking their flesh while silent seeds cracked and sprouted silently in the underground.

A veil of fog wrapped the woods like a cocoon, protecting the dark blossom. A fluff of dark concealing the life occurring, the power growing and opening. A distant cloud nobody dared to near, from the other side of the desert encircling it, for fear that legend may have been history.

***

Only the dead ever saw the blood roses. Only the chosen dead glided across the barren land, crossed the veil like a spider web and entered the forest, summoned by the promise of a gift. Their eyes brightened by the pang of the flowers' scent, a pang of emotion as hair lifted with soulful wind and, suddenly, they were alive again. Petals rippled like crimson puddles as they dipped their fingertips and traced the shape of perfection on their lips—filled of tender flesh to kiss and die in, dressed head to toe in beauty.

***

As *the* time descends, the web tears.

Light as butterflies the chosen permeate back into the outer world, blending into the shadows, until they allow themselves to be seen—striking vulnerable hearts with dark, eternal love. Like all flowers they too shall wither, when the blood forest crumbles to ash—a black scar in the heart of the desert, shaped as a perfect rose—only visible to those who carry a scar of equal shape in their iris, carved by the indelible first-sight that would ever change them.

But by then they will have served their purpose.

Those who will lift the wind and reveal the rose under the loose sand.

A circle of hands around it; an enchanted circle of beauty casting the new order of things.

A STOLEN HEART

By R.J. Meldrum

The police weren't interested, nor was the municipality. We dared not contact the media for fear of being swamped by kooks. In desperation, we contacted the local university. A Professor and a research student poked around for a couple of days, measuring and taking samples. The data was normal, and they soon lost interest. The Professor said it must be some sort of unique, unexplainable, localised phenomenon. That, remarked Sarah within earshot of the departing university team, was already bloody obvious.

And so, we were left with our own unique, unexplainable, localised phenomenon. The pond in the paddock next to the house was frozen. In August.

Sarah and I stood at the edge of the pond, gazing down at the frozen water. There wasn't anything to say. We'd moved to the farm a month ago, it had been my uncle's. Unknown to me, he'd left it to me in his will. Sarah and I had decided to move in, rather than sell it. Urban living didn't suit us and the opportunity to move to a hundred-acre farm appealed to us both. We packed up our belongings and headed to the country, excited about our new rural life. It was perfect until last week, when we noticed the pond had frozen.

I glanced back at the house. It was constructed from the local stone and was impressively solid. The thick walls and slate roof could easily withstand the cold winters and strong winds that were typical of the region. My uncle, a confirmed bachelor, had raised sheep here for decades; they were the only animals that thrived on these desolate moors.

I saw Daisy standing at her bedroom window, her face serious. She was a very serious child, despite being only four. We hadn't let her near the pond, ignoring her pleas to go skating. The university team had tested it and confirmed the ice was composed of water and nothing else, but we both felt uneasy about letting our daughter close to it. Water shouldn't freeze when the air temperature is twenty degrees Celsius.

I glanced up again at the house. Daisy was gone from her window.

"Better go and check on her," said Sarah.

I found her in the cellar. It wasn't a livable space; it was dirty, cramped and damp, still full of my uncle's junk. She knew she wasn't allowed in there and normally she would never have dared enter, but we'd both noticed she'd been acting strangely since the pond froze. She was standing in the far corner with her back to me. As I stepped onto the dirt floor, I felt a sudden, unseen presence. I'm not a particularly imaginative person, but I knew that this was supernatural. There was nothing to see, but I had the sensation of being surrounded by a malevolent force. It swirled around me. I was suddenly aware I couldn't move; the presence had incapacitated me, somehow stopping my muscles from moving. I felt a growing tightness in my chest; it was getting hard to breathe.

Daisy spoke without looking around.

"Don't. He's my daddy. He's not that other man, the one you're afraid of."

My muscles were suddenly released. I felt the presence step back from me. I rushed forward and grabbed Daisy, but she was unperturbed. Before I could ask her what the hell just happened, she looked at me.

"You need to open the wall, daddy. She wants you to."

"Who?"

"Her. The girl who speaks to me. The girl who froze the pond."

She pointed at the wall.

"There."

I did as my daughter asked. The bricks were old, crumbling. I removed two of them easily enough and discovered a battered metal box. I took it out of the wall and opened it with a sense of dread. It contained a tiny dried, shrivelled, burgundy object and a sealed envelope. We immediately called the authorities.

Forensic examination identified the object as a human heart, belonging to a child of around ten years old. The letter, written by my uncle, told the story of what had happened. He had taken a child and drowned her in the pond. There was no emotion in the words he had written, he gave no explanation for his deed. Excavations in our cellar found the rest of her remains. She was identified as Maggie MacPherson, a local girl who disappeared in 1966. My uncle had lived in that house for fifty years, with the body of a child interred in the cellar and her heart in a box. I couldn't even start to guess what had been wrong with him. I wondered why he'd left the house to me.

Sarah and I spent many hours discussing what had happened. The only reasonable explanation was that we had been visited by the spirit of the dead child. It was possible Daisy's presence in that lonely, cold house had woken Maggie from her restless slumber. Maggie must have thought my uncle had taken another victim, that he was about to kill again. She had frozen the pond so he couldn't drown Daisy.

On the day that Maggie's remains were removed from the cellar, we stood next to the hearse and paid our respects as the tiny coffin was loaded. I placed my hand onto the wood and silently thanked her for protecting my daughter. The pond thawed the same day.

First published in *Sirens Call eZine*, 2016

HEY SIRI

By Jodi Jensen

Chloe snapped her seat belt and started her car. "Hey, Siri, send text message to Sam."

"*What do you want to say?*" the robotic voice asked.

"Have you boarded yet?"

"*Message sent.*"

As she backed out of her driveway, her phone chimed, letting her know he'd answered. "Hey, Siri, read last text."

"*I found your latest message from Sam... Boarding now, will text you when I land. See you soon... Would you like to reply?*"

"No." In less than two hours, she'd be picking him up from the airport. This living-in-different-states was hard, but they were making it work. They'd been taking turns flying out to see each other, and though it was her turn to go there, he'd insisted on coming here for Valentine's Day, saying he had a surprise for her. She smiled at the thought, then cranked her music and settled in for the drive.

As she made her way into the city an hour later, she merged from the highway to the Interstate and was cut-off by a semi. Her car skidded onto the shoulder, spun around, then dropped into the ditch.

She sat in a daze, staring at the smoke rising from the hood. After a moment, she blinked and glanced around. The semi was nowhere to be seen. She smacked the steering wheel over and over. "God dammit son of a bitch!" The jerk had run her clear off the road and hadn't even bothered to stop.

She reached for her phone, but her hands were shaking too bad to pick it up. "Hey, Siri, send text message to Sam."

"*What do you want to say?*"

"I had a small accident, calling for a tow, will be there as soon as I can."

"*Message sent.*"

She leaned her head back against the seat and took a couple deep breaths. "Hey, Siri, call nearest towing company."

Silence.

She tried again with the same result. Now that her hands were steadier, she picked up her phone, intending to search for a tow truck. The screen stayed black when she pushed the home button. She tried the side button, then finally tried turning it off, but nothing changed. Just a black screen.

What the hell? It worked a minute ago.

As a last-ditch effort, she tried one more time. "Hey, Siri, send text message to

Sam."

"*What do you want to say?*"

Her breath caught, it worked! "Call me as soon as you get this."

"*Message sent.*"

Maybe asking to locate and call a towing company was too ambiguous, so she switched tactics. "Hey, Siri, call 911."

Total silence.

"Oh, for fuck's sake," she muttered. Grabbing her phone, she yanked her door open and got out to see the damage. The front corner was smashed in so far that the hood was bent upward at a weird angle and part of the motor was visible. Part of the *smoking* motor.

That can't be good.

She glanced at her phone, intending to

call for help, but the screen was still black. From where she stood in the ditch, she could hear the traffic on the freeway, but couldn't see anything. With no other choice, she climbed the steep embankment.

When she reached the top, she stood back a little, right on the edge of the gravel, and waved her arms at the vehicles speeding by.

Not even one of them slowed down.

A wave of heated anger washed over her. Was chivalry dead? Where were all the good Samaritans?

Overhead, a plane flew low as it approached the airport.

Maybe it was Sam's.

"Hey, Siri, send text message to Sam."

"What do you want to say?"

Her throat tightened as she spoke. "Sam, it's me. I'm stuck on the side of the road and my phone is wacked. It's not letting me make any calls."

"*Message sent.*"

She cleared her throat and swallowed hard. Damn, she wished she had a drink of water. "Hey, Siri, send text message to Sam."

"*What do you want to say?*"

"I'm on the southbound side of the Interstate, I can see the airport exit sign from where I'm at. Please call 911 for me, then get an Uber or something."

"*Message sent.*"

Chloe glanced at the phone in her hand, but the screen remained black. She stuffed the useless thing in her pocket and waved her arms over her head at the steady stream of traffic passing her by.

After a few more minutes and still no one had stopped, she decided to hike back down to her car for her water bottle. She'd taken her first steps down the embankment when her phone chimed.

Sam!

When she pulled it out of her pocket to find the screen still dark, she was barely phased.

"Hey, Siri, read last text."

"*I found your latest message from Sam... Stay where you are Chloe, I called for an ambulance. Help is on the way. I grabbed a cab and I'll be there as fast as I can... Would you like to reply?*"

Before she could answer, her damaged

phone chimed again.

"Hey, Siri, read last text."

"I found your latest message from Sam... I love you, baby... Would you like to reply?"

"Yes." She sat down in the dirt.

"What do you want to say?"

Her body trembled in relief. "I love you, too, Sam. Please hurry."

"Message sent."

Within minutes, she heard the wail of sirens and scrambled to her feet.

Her stomach dropped when the ambulance drove right by, despite her waving like crazy. She kicked the dirt and was about to let out a string of cuss words, when the emergency vehicle slowed down, then pulled over by the airport exit sign.

The reverse lights came on and the ambulance backed up on the shoulder, finally stopping by the skid marks from her car.

Two men jumped out and took off running down into the ditch, yelling her name.

"I'm right here!" She ran after the paramedics, beyond thrilled to see them, even as she called them idiots under her breath.

Just then another car stopped, and she turned to see a bright yellow cab.

Her heart leapt as she changed direction, wanting nothing more than to be safe in Sam's arms. A broad smile curved her lips when he opened the back door and got out. She ran toward him, but he turned away, scanning the roadside, then looking at his phone.

"Sam!" Another semi whizzed by and she yelled louder to be heard over the noise. "Sam! I'm here!"

He still didn't see her but looked down and tapped on his phone instead.

A few more seconds and she was in front of him. "Sam?"

From behind her, a man yelled, and Sam took off running.

What—

Her phone chimed.

She ignored it and ran after Sam. "Wait!"

He half stumbled, half slid down the steep slope where her car was, screaming her name as he went.

Chloe chased him until her car came into view.

The paramedics were prying the door open and calling her name.

As the vehicle jostled, a mass of matted and bloody hair lolled against the window.

She froze.

Her phone chimed again.

Sam crumpled to the ground beside the car, his head in his hands.

She glanced from him, to her phone, then said in a tight voice, "Hey, Siri, read last text."

"*I found your latest message from Sam... Baby, where are you? I'm here... Would you like to reply?*"

"Yes," she muttered, even as she

stared at her wrecked car and the love of her life sobbing on the ground next to it.

"*What do you want to say?*"

"I'm here, too, Sam. I'm right here."

"*Message sent.*"

She watched in awe as he jumped when his phone chimed.

He glanced at the screen, then looked around in disbelief before reading the message. "Chloe?"

"I'm here, Sam," she whispered. The pain and grief on his face broke her heart as realisation dawned.

She gripped her phone a little tighter. "Hey, Siri..."

SHARDS

By Kimberly Rei

Lions haunt my dreams. Two legged, sliding through darkness, made of wisped shadow. Their edges are tattered, but only a fool would mistake them for weak. Ancient, primordial hunters learned from these wraiths.

At the scrape of bladed claws and the snap of a leathery multi-fallen tail, I flee. Across asphalt savannahs, into the depths of the forest. Rebar trees clad in concrete leaves, a sanctuary broken and crumbling.

There is no wind to calm the heat or muffle sound. My feet land heavy as I pick my way around destruction, seeking desperate shelter where there is none to be found.

Leonine stars claimed my birth and bid me worship the sun. Pernicious will lead me to the night and the moon. Both betray dreams. And as I shiver against a wall as ruined as my harmony, an ebony light stirs. Neither moon nor sun dare reveal themselves here. This is no place for the natural.

Sandalwood and orchid, rich soil and petrichor. Arctic tendrils stagger through stirred dust. Razored talons tap my stone haven.

My soul screams for the waking world.

MEYER HOUSE

By Gabriella Balcom

Phineas rolled his eyes as the faint scratching sound slowly travelled from behind him to his right, growing louder as it moved. "That's lame," he muttered, not bothering to look. He glanced at his wristwatch, frowned, and quickly left his room.

"The Meyer family moved from Pennsylvania to Texas in 1847," the tour guide shared a few minutes later. "The father, George, was a wealthy merchant, and he and his wife, Portia, had two daughters, Karina and Tabitha. The Meyers built this home in 1848. Karina turned sixteen the following year, and fell in love with Alistair, the housekeeper's son. He was seventeen. They wanted to marry, but Karina's parents refused. They wanted her to marry someone from a higher socioeconomic class, so they planned a match between her and the son of a successful financier."

"Did Karina and Alistair run away

together?" a woman to Phineas' right asked. "I love happy endings."

"According to lore, that's exactly what they'd planned to do," the guide replied. "But Karina's parents found out and were determined to prevent it from happening. Her father locked her in her room and had slats of wood nailed over the outside of her window. Alistair's mother was fired, and she and her son were kicked out of the house, then escorted out of town by a constable. When Karina found out her beloved was gone, she hung herself in her bedroom."

"That's the one I'm in, isn't it?" a woman asked, her voice squeaking.

"Yes," the guide confirmed. "Throughout the years, she's been heard wailing, pounding on the door, and calling for Alistair. Some visitors have even seen her body hanging from the light fixture…"

Several of the people staying in the house voiced sympathy or expressed how they, too, hoped to see and hear the ghost.

Phineas almost scoffed, but clamped his lips together, stopping himself. It wouldn't do to give away the reason for his presence; people would find out soon enough.

"Shh. I want to hear this," he told a loud talker after the guide started his spiel again, saying a little girl had drowned in a tub, and a family had been murdered in another room. Supposedly, a man whose stock crashed had climbed onto the roof of the house, leaping to his death, and another had drowned in a nearby pond.

The stories were interesting and based on actual events, according to the research Phineas had done before coming. But the "haunted" parts were sheer drivel, as far as he was concerned—exaggerations and lies to ramp up the Meyer House's reputation as one of the most haunted places in Texas.

Once the tour ended, he had a quick lunch before returning to his room, planning to take a short nap before doing a bit of exploration. He pulled off a shoe, flinching when he saw movement from the corner of his right eye. He glanced toward it, recoiling as a roach scurried from underneath the dresser. Phineas jumped up, stomped on the floor, and the thing vanished.

Eyebrows raised, the man wondered at first if he'd imagined the bug, but reasoned it must've slipped between floorboards.

Warm air blew on the back of Phineas' neck, and he whirled, seeing no vent or opening behind him. He examined both the wall and floor, found no hole of any kind, and frowned.

Then a blast of air, icy-cold this time, hit the right side of his face. He blinked rapidly when more blew into his eyes. Something cool touched his arm, even though nothing was there.

"Not bad," he murmured grudgingly. "So you have a few good tricks up your sleeves, huh?" All thoughts of napping gone, he jotted down notes about what he'd experienced, along with possible explanations for how each thing had been staged.

Screams in the distance brought him surging to his feet, and he blinked a few times, fuzzy-headed. He realised he must've dozed off after all and charged out the door and down the hall, almost bumping into the woman who'd rented the Karina room. Her face was flushed, chest heaving as she babbled incoherently.

Once she calmed down enough to form words, she revealed, "I took a bath, and when I came out, she was standing at the door—Karina, I mean. Her back was to me, and she was crying and crying like her heart was broken. I said, 'I'm so sorry, you poor dear,' and she turned around like she heard me. But then she changed from a sweet, sad girl into a rotting corpse and came straight at me. I thought she was going to kill me or something."

Phineas got the woman's permission to look around her room, and concluded images had probably been projected from a vent high on the wall, facing the door. However, when he used his pocketknife to remove the cover, all he found was thick dust which showed no evidence of having been disturbed.

The rest of the evening passed uneventfully, except for one couple reporting a strange chill in one corner of their room, despite the rest being warmer.

***

The next day

Chest growing tighter by the second,

Phineas struggled to breathe. Something was around his neck, cutting off his air supply. He clawed with his fingers at what felt like a cord or rope, trying to loosen the thing, but it merely tightened. He wasn't in bed, but dangling from the ceiling fan above it, spinning round and round.

"How could you leave me, Alistair?" a female voice whispered, ragged with anguish and tears.

Phineas' eyes popped open, and he sat up, gasping for air, looking wildly around the room. It took a few moments before he realised he was in bed. Even though he knew he'd been dreaming, it took awhile for his heart to stop racing. The thing around his neck felt so real—just as real as hanging and being unable to breathe.

He wondered if the power of suggestion had caused everything he'd experienced, or if there was a darker explanation. Certain drugs could cause hallucinations, and he'd eaten a meal in the house, since they were included in the cost of the room.

Phineas decided on the spot not to eat there anymore. "You may fool me once," he groused. "Maybe even twice. But that's it."

He waited till 2:45 AM, hoping everyone was asleep, and quietly left his room, heading for the basement. It was one of the few places the visitors had been told was off-limits; the staff claiming the central heat and air system was having problems. The door was locked, a sign on it proclaiming, "KEEP OUT," but he was able to pick the lock.

It didn't take Phineas long to conclude he'd wasted his time. The basement was empty except for the heat and air system and a few boxes of towels, soaps, and other supplies. He found no sound equipment, cameras, projectors, or anything to prove the staff were behind the paranormal experiences.

That left the attic.

He scowled once he'd gotten there and looked around, though. Despite him finding electronics, they were just old TVs, a microwave, and a couple of ancient fans—nothing even remotely like a sophisticated set-up to fool people into thinking the place was haunted.

A very disgruntled Phineas slipped quietly back into his room. He gasped when he saw a spider on his chest, knocked it off, stomped on it repeatedly, and glared at the body. He sighed, shoulders drooping, knowing his editor would stomp all over him if he returned with no story, or if he concluded the allegedly paranormal events were real.

He perked up when an idea popped into his head. If drugs were being added to visitors' meals, surely they'd be kept in the kitchen. And, he could look in the manager's office; it might hold some type of records which could help him.

Phineas was surprised to find the office wasn't locked. It held scant files, which he leafed through, finding nothing useful. The kitchen was just as disappointing, with no drugs anywhere—at least, none that he found.

Rubbing his forehead, he glanced around the kitchen, wondering if he'd missed something. Maybe the innocent labels on the containers like salt and pepper concealed other ingredients.

A scratching sound came from his left, similar to what he'd heard in his room the day he'd arrived, and he perked up. However, he took an involuntary step backward when the noise came from all directions at the same time. It intensified, a low growling accompanying it, and he backed away more, bumping into a wall.

Something shoved him violently from behind, almost making him lose his balance. But he managed to stay on his feet, and couldn't keep from grinning. *Now* he understood what was going on. Some of the walls weren't solid. Confident about his conclusion, he stalked toward the wall his back had hit, touching it. But, no matter how high or low he reached, the wall was solid.

Phineas gritted his teeth, so infuriated he could've chewed nails. Miserable frauds. He didn't know how they'd done it, but he'd figure it out if it was the last thing he did.

"Lastlastlastlastlastlastlastlastlast," voices around him whispered, and he didn't even realise they'd plucked the word from his mind.

"Shut up," Phineas retorted, dead

certain there were microphones hidden here and there. Did the staff know he was employed by a newspaper? Even if they knew what he was doing there, it didn't matter, because he wasn't backing down. He'd come to debunk the alleged paranormal activities, and debunk them he would. If anything, he was more determined now than ever.

A man's head appeared across the room, but was gone within seconds, followed by a doll which floated toward him, also disappearing. A woman in white stepped out of the wall beside him, and he jumped, flinching again when she sank into the floor.

Hands came from the walls, vanishing almost immediately. Two extended from the ceiling, attached to impossibly long arms.

Phineas backed away, but refused to run, certain he was on the verge of discovering something important. The Meyer House staff wouldn't have gone to all this trouble for any other reason; he was sure of it.

Blood began seeping from the fingers above him, trickling onto the floor. Impressed despite himself, Phineas stooped to touch what he was sure was another projected image. These special effects were great, but fake, nonetheless.

However, when he touched the expanding red puddle, his fingers came away dripping red. Taking a sniff, he discovered the substance smelled like coppery blood, and his heart began beating faster. Uncertain what to do, but knowing he had to do something, he grabbed one of the dangling hands. It resisted, then came loose so abruptly he lost his balance and landed on his bottom, next to the arm.

He stood, examining the arm, turning it over in his hands, stunned to realise it felt as solid and real as his own but stunk like rotting flesh. Maggots oozed from the skin, crawling onto his hands, and he couldn't hold back a shriek. He dropped the arm and it vanished.

Something he couldn't see grabbed his left shoulder, and he had to fight to get loose.

Phineas couldn't stay calm, despite his former determination to find the answers.

Sheer terror filled him, and he panicked. He fled the kitchen, running down the hall toward the front door as fast as he could, but hands shot out of the walls on either side of him. He managed to evade some, but not all. Several grabbed him, and he yelled for help when he couldn't get loose. He was still screaming when they pulled him into a wall, all sound ceasing.

He stepped out within seconds, face expressionless.

Voices rang out from everywhere as the other people staying at Meyer House came out of their rooms to see what was going on, along with the manager and live-in employees.

"Who was yelling?" a male guest demanded.

"I don't know," the manager replied, eyes troubled as he glanced around them. "People, please step outside while my staff and I look around."

"No way," the man replied. "Whoever that was sounded like he was being murdered."

"I think we should all stick together," a woman offered.

"All right," the manager said. "Follow me then." He, the staff, and the guests trooped from room to room, but found nothing amiss, and when they did a headcount, no one was missing.

***

One week later

"His employer said he didn't return to work," Officer Bellamy stated. "And he was supposed to a few days ago."

"I don't know what to say," Jon, the manager of Meyer House, said. "Phineas Wayne paid for a week, then left." He retrieved the old ledger from the foyer and flipped through pages, then handed the book to Bellamy, pointing to an entry. "I keep electronic records, too, but this is a book I leave out for guests. They can list their names and addresses to be added to our mailing list, or write comments. The day Phineas checked out, he wrote this and dated it."

Bellamy read the entry, which was complimentary, snapped a picture with his phone, and returned the ledger to Jon. "Did he mention any plans to go somewhere else?"

"Not that I recall, but quite a few people come through. You're welcome to talk to my staff if you want. They might remember something I don't."

At the police station, Officer Bellamy leaned back in his chair. "As far as I can tell, no one had any cause to hurt the man. His editor said he went to Meyer House to prove the hauntings were fake, but no one there knew. Even if they did, he'd talked to his editor a couple times and hadn't found anything to back up his suspicions about the place."

"I've checked with the surrounding businesses," his partner, Officer Yurtz replied. "Two of them have cameras and surveillance. I got one set of recordings and the other set will be delivered soon."

***

Four hours later

"There he is, leaving Meyer House," Bellamy said, pointing at the screen.

"You sure?" Yurtz demanded, rewinding the tape, leaning in for a closer look. "Never mind. You're right. He was facing the camera when he talked to the cab driver."

"Get a load of his eyes," Bellamy commented, chuckling. "They look like they're yellow and glowing."

"That's neat. A trick of the light."

"Well, his editor was wrong, thinking the folks at Meyer House did away with him. We can see for ourselves he's healthy there, and leaving on his own two feet."

"I guess he made other plans without

telling his boss. Maybe he couldn't face that he didn't find anything."

Bellamy nodded. "We'll check with the cabbie to see where he was dropped off, even though it's a waste of our time."

"A *total* waste." Yurtz snorted. "I'm sure he's fine, wherever he is."

A THING OF BEAUTY

By Carole McDonnell

When Father James McLaren opened his eyes from the grand sleep of death, it was not upon the heavenly throne room. His was not the celestial vision of the enthroned deity, but a bag of hay seeds and a pile of manure. He rose from the wheelbarrow in which his body rested and took the measure of his situation.

The first observation was that he was not in hospital garb. Instead, he was wearing his clerical collar and all the accoutrement of his calling. His right pocket even contained a bottle of anointing oil and a small cross.

The second observation was that he was in no pain whatsoever and he could breathe like a kid of sixteen. All of this was remarkable because the last thing he knew of himself was that some ten minutes earlier—and for about eight years—he had been killing himself with alcohol and cigarettes. But now, the cirrhosis and the lung cancer were apparently gone.

His thoughts turned from himself to his surroundings. He was obviously in a shed or a barn. He had awakened to find a horse's rear end in his face and had been thrown onto a pile of manure in a wheelbarrow.

Obviously, the Almighty had a sense of humour.

"But He has granted me mercy!" Father James exclaimed, shouting. Then, more intimately, "You, Dear Lord, have granted this thieving, lusting, blind-eye-turning priest a second chance! I have been saved from the pains of Hell. Thank you. Thank you. Thank you."

Several thin streams of light filtered through cracks in the wooden walls. A mid-afternoon sun, James thought. The air in the barn felt fresh but cold and the coldness nipped at his nose and at his dark brown skin. *I need a coat*, he thought and studied his long brown fingers, now no longer the fingers of a dying eighty-six year-old man. Still, they were almost numbed from the cold. I most definitely need need need gloves!

It was then that it occurred to him that perhaps he was not entirely free. After all, as far as he knew, this sort of thing was quite rare. Unless it had always been part of the Almighty's repertoire to translate mob priests from hell to barns, surely some penance was necessary. It was then that he thought to ask, "Lord, what will you have me to do?"

The thought came to him that he

should look in his left shirt pocket, and this he did. Looking, he found a note neatly-written in the finest cursive imaginable, "Go and build me a school for orphans. All your paperwork is in order."

"Paperwork?" he muttered, and then searched the left pocket of his pants. Finding several pieces of paper rolled together, he opened them and saw that they were from the diocese of Maryland.

The hoofbeats of several horses outside the barn, and what he assumed was neighing, momentarily startled him. But he kept his mind, keener than ever because it was freed from pain, on the task he had been given.

"Orphans?" he said aloud to himself. "How pure and good is that!" It would certainly be better than turning a blind eye to murderous mob bosses, ignoring their cruelty to their fellow men and mistresses, and saying pious empty words over their corpses. A horse outside neighed, and Father James looked up at the barn door. He brushed off the remaining manure from his clothing. *I think that was neighing. Or it might be a whinny*, he thought. *But what do I know of horses?* He flicked some bits of horse manure out of his afro and walked outside.

The first thing he saw were two white cowboys. They were standing beside two of the most beautiful horses Father James had ever seen.

"How majestic and wonderful are your creations, Oh God!" Father James said.

Then he turned to look down the unpaved streets. It's something out of a movie set, he thought, intrigued. God dropped me into a movie set? Ah, perhaps he wants me to take care of Hollywood street kids and runaways.

I'd be good at that, he told himself. Kids liked him, and he himself had been a runaway back in the day.

His gaze returned to the men, and he looked up at the face of the older of the two. "This a movie set?" he asked.

They exchanged bewildered looks. At last, the younger one—a blond teenager with sweat dripping from his brow—said, "You a priest or something?"

Father James smiled, extended his parchment-like resume toward the men.

"That I am. From the diocese of Maryland. Apparently."

The men glanced at each other, then at the priest, again with evident bewilderment. "You a priest?" the young one asked, so incredulously that even the ever-jaded Father James almost began to worry. "A real priest? They're making Blacks priests now?"

The older cowboy removed his ten-gallon hat and wiped sweat from his brow. "What you doin' here?" he asked James. "This ain't free territory. Priest or not, them bounty hunters find you...you gonna be taken to some plantation."

Ah, James thought. *This is getting interesting.*

Having been dragged into mob truces

and been surprised more than once by confessions of murder and torment, James was never one to be flustered. "And might I ask you where we might be and what the year of our Dear Lord is?"

"Father," the older cowboy said, "it is the year of our Lord, 1850. And you're in Louisiana."

"Ah," said Father James, "that could be problematical." Only fifteen minutes ago, he had been on his deathbed in 2015, New York, surrounded by loving and weeping congregants. A place which now seemed a hundred times safer than a plantation in the antebellum southwest.

"How come you don't know where you at?" the kid asked. "You been imbibing? Or you get conked on the head or something?"

"Neither," James answered, and because his high school days were sixty years in the past and more than a century in the future, he added, "And where, may I ask, is the nearest free state?"

"Kansas," the teenage boy said.

Now James was not one to miss anything. One of the largest heroin sellers on the East Coast had even called him "whip-smart." So it quickly occurred to him that his meeting with these two men could not have been an accident. Surely, any other meeting with ranch hands, or white men in general, from the past would not be so typically courteous. "Tell me," he asked, "are you two...abolitionists?"

"We're Quakers," the older man

answered. "And I suppose you could call us abolitionists."

"But don't call it too loud," the younger man said.

"Ah, Quakers!" Father James looked about what he supposed was the town square—a wide, dust-blown expanse, dotted with about forty one or two story buildings. For the first time, he felt somewhat nervous about his strange situation. "How wonderfully precipitous and timely! Could it be that we are destined to meet?"

The two cowboys looked at each other, then at the priest. "Are you thinking of the Underground Railroad to Canada?" the older man.

James thought for a moment. As he

studied the leather coats of the men, he felt a chill coming on. *The Almighty could at least have given me a coat,* he whined inwardly, then turned his attention once again to his rescuers. "I've never liked Canadians," he said at last, and rubbed his shoulder. "I'll stay here. This is where the Lord sent me."

The older man squinted; the younger bit his bottom lip. It was clear they thought he was seriously nuts.

"I'm to build an orphanage," he told them. "One for all races. A great rainbow coalition." He paused. "But tell me, what might your names be?"

"The name's Jacob Brackner," the older man said. "And that's my boy, Joseph."

"Glad to meet you. But do you know...I am seriously hungry." Then he quipped, "Apparently being raised from the dead does that." They looked at him quizzically. "Long story," he said. "Oh...and don't worry about giving me a ride. I can walk. Only ride very slowly so I can follow and not get lost?"

Father James had always been skilful at getting himself invited to dinner. But it was quite true: being resurrected from the dead tended to make a person ravenously hungry. And with the added dimension of time travel and travelling back to the past...well, he could eat a horse.

"Best you not walk," the older man said, a warning in his voice. "Or are you forgetting where you are? Just you wait right there. The missus will be coming with the wagon soon."

And so she did. She arrived driving a two-horse covered wagon—and if she blinked or paused on seeing James, the good pastor didn't notice. Like Jonah of old, James was an animal lover, and he had fallen instantly in love with a fat and docile hog stumbling about in the back of the wagon.

James helped them remove several large bags of grain from the general store barn and then followed them to the butcher shop, where James' new friend was slaughtered before his tear-filled eyes.

Dressed as he was, it wasn't long before James became a bit of a spectacle. Several folks, including the town drunk, gathered about to watch the little—James was a mere five foot three—black priest.

He walked toward one man who was eyeing him cautiously. "Father James McLaren," James said and extended his right hand. "Apparently, you folks have never seen a Catholic before."

"He's got his papers on him," the boy quickly chimed in.

The man grinned to himself, then walked away without shaking James' hand.

"What papers?" James asked the boy, who was looking even more worried than before.

"Papers saying you're free," the kid answered. "Not that it matters if he finds you alone."

"Ah!" James said, then he shouted at

the man's back, "I'm actually a rather nice guy!"

"You best learn who you should joke with, Father," the older man said. "That one there is Albert. He's our marshall. He also owns a large farm around here with 'bout maybe 20 slaves. The wrong man for you to seek friendship with. And come to think of it, your pleasantries could leave you and me and my family dead. So, best keep your head down and your humour even lower while I figure out how to explain you."

"Explaining having a Black man in your wagon?" James asked.

"No," the man answered with a wry smile, "explaining what I'm doing with a Catholic."

"Either way, you're in trouble, I suspect," James said.

He truly suspected trouble. And he knew he should be afraid. Yet, he could not help himself. He was alive! He was hale, hearty, and free from pain. He wanted to weep with joy. Surely, the feeling of a healthy body was one of the banal wonders given by God for humans to enjoy!

So James worked as he had not done in years, hauling and dragging and lifting—and all the time resisting the urge to weep with joy at his returned health.

When the family finished their shopping, James joined them in their wagon, sitting atop a bag of flour, some horse feed, a tin of salt, a few remains from his lost friend, and a yard of blue gingham.

As the wagon turned from town toward the wide expanse of scrub and faded grasslands, James looked out at the town square disappearing behind him: under the darkening mid-afternoon sky, Albert was watching him.

***

Having eaten two plates full of beans, a hunk of salted bacon and rattlesnake, and five boiled buckwheat dumplings, and having drunk three mugs of sarsaparilla root beer, Father James was licking his fingers enthusiastically when he realised his hostess, a greying matron, was looking down at him with both pity and worry. Although soft curls framed what could only be called a sweet face, James suspected Mistress Brackner could and would wield her frying pan with the same power and precision her rancher husband had used in dispatching the rattlesnake they'd just eaten.

So this is what a frontier woman looks like, he thought, stocky, fatigued, grim, but somewhat sweet. Then, because his hosts were all studiously looking at him, he said, "You're a mighty fine cook, Mistress Brackner. Mighty fine." James had watched an awful lot of westerns in his younger days and the lingo had slowly been returning to him as he ate, as were all his memories of his younger, nobler self. He had to admit that the westerns had had a good influence on him. They had taught him about chivalry, machismo, and being a straight-shooter. Murdering Injuns and shufflin' Black folks notwithstanding.

"But to the matter at hand," he said. "My orphanage. Where should I build it? In Kansas, you say? And will you help me get there, Rancher Brackner?"

"I ain't no rancher, Father, and gimme a minute to think."

The boy glanced at the window. "Now that they know you're here, they'll most likely come a'visiting. To see if you're a real priest."

"Not that that matters," the missus said, then added, "You full?"

Father James tapped his stomach. "Quite." He looked about the room and toward the mirror. He'd seen the mirror when he first entered, but had avoided looking into it. It was not every day that one encountered one's younger, twenty-year-old self. But was he, in fact, twenty?

So even while eating the most fulfilling meal ever, he had had his mind on his former face. What did he look like? What face was the Brackner family seeing?

He stood up, bowed, and said a prayer of thanksgiving. He noticed it again as he had the first time. The look that sometimes came over people when a priest offered a prayer. These are holy people, he thought. And he wondered at their salt of the earth goodness. He had not seen it in ages, not since he got so sick he couldn't go to the parish church.

And even before that. When he was still officiating, he would only see that love of holiness in the eyes of the little old women at Mass. Not in the eyes of the mob guys, though. Made guys didn't really care about holiness.

He walked to the mirror with his eyes closed, not caring that the collective gaze of his hosts were on him. When he knew he stood before it, he opened his eyes. In spite of himself, he gasped. There he was: his younger self.

It had been a handsome—some might have said "beautiful"—face. And years of unscrupulousness and duplicity had not marred it. Age had, however. But even when he reached the golden age of eighty and had been overly-wined and overly-dined by the powerful politicians, gangsters, merchants, and bishops, the beauty was still there.

"I'm like Dorian Gray," he said aloud to himself, and then to the watching family. "All my wrinkles have melted away."

"How wrinkled could a man of twenty be?" the much-wrinkled Missus Brackner asked.

"Indeed," Father James said. "Quite true."

For he was thinking of wrinkled souls and not wrinkled skin. And his soul was wrinkled indeed. And why had so many creases marked his soul over the years? The answer was clear enough. Truly, it had always been clear. But those months spent on his deathbed and the unending procession of thieves, murderers, shyster lawyers, and greedy politicians all bringing larger and larger flower arrangements had made it all all all too clear: Because I wanted to be seen as understanding, as patient, as likable.

"It is a disgusting thing to be well-liked," he said, half to himself.

The boy looked up at him. "What's that you say?"

Father James began to answer, but a knock sounded on the door, and outside the house a voice called, "Open up, Brackner. It's me, Marshall Caine. We hear you got an escaped slave in there. I've come to take him in."

Inside the house, all grew still as everyone froze. Jacob Brackner rose from his seat. He put his right index finger to his lips, pointed to the floor. Immediately, the family lifted the heavy table and kicked away the rug underneath it. At James' feet was the opening to a trap-door. He knew without them speaking a word that he had to climb down it. This he quickly did and they closed it over him, along with the plate and cup he'd been using. He heard the rug being slid over the floor, then the table being put back into place.

"Brackner! You hear me?" the voice called again. "You opening this door, or should I break it down?"

"No need to do that, Marshall," Brackner's voice answered.

"Is this what it was like?" Father James asked as he looked up at the floor above his head. "To have the dirt over my head? And will I die here now? Was this only a short reprieve?"

He was not afraid. On the contrary, he was preternaturally calm. Even when, above him, the front door of the cabin creaked open slowly.

"What took you so long?" a gruff male voice demanded. Harsh footsteps—the booted feet of five or six men—trampled into the room of the cabin. "Where is he?"

"He?" Missus Brackner answered. "You mean the Black priest? We sent him on his way."

"Search the place!" Then, "Boy! If you know what's good for you, you'll come on out from where you're hiding!"

Father James did not budge. Instead, a memory came to his mind. It had lain in his mind, long-forgotten. One of the hitmen, who regularly came to him for confession, had talked about the giddy joy he felt when his prey was hiding from him.

"It's the funniest thing, Father," the guy had said. "It's like...my blood gets all...I dunno. I get excited like. And I can smell blood. I can smell the guy's fear, you know. And it's like...it's like a thrill. And I love it so much. Weird, uh?"

"Not especially," Father James had answered.

Because he had heard that kind of confession before. From Black gangsters, Italian mafia guys, Russian hitmen. He was well-known for giving them penances, which they always completed. They'd come back and tell him how clean they felt. After they'd given some money to an orphanage. After they'd secretly arranged for money to be given to the widow of their prey. After they'd filled some poor churches' coffers. But they'd never changed. The thrill of killing would come back. And now Father James pondered the fact that he himself was now prey, that he was now actively disliked.

He clasped his hands together around his knee and waited, remembering the names of the many preys he had heard of. Above him, the marshall and his officers searched, then hollered when they could not find him.

"He's still round here somewhere," the marshall said. "In the barn, maybe."

"I tell you, he's gone," the missus said.

James heard a chair being pulled across the floor and surmised that Albert had decided to sit a spell.

Apparently, that was exactly what Albert had done. It was pretty evident to James that the guy sensed his prey nearby and wouldn't be leaving anytime soon. Like many of the bullies James had met, he was intent on showing his power. Manspreading, probably, James thought, and snorting up dinner like addicts snorting cocaine.

The day drew to its close and Marshall Albert was still sitting there, schmoozing and making threatening small talk. Taking up space. Taking up time. So James sat in that pit, prey, fearing to move and waiting for his enemy to smell him out, as the hitmen used to say.

As he sat there, cramped, the thought

suddenly occurred to him that perhaps he had indeed died and was in Hell. For all the times I turned a blind eye, he thought. Because I wanted to be liked.

But then a worse thought came: perhaps he had yet to die. Maybe he had not died at all, but even now was in the process of dying on his deathbed in Catholic Metropolitan Hospital, and the entire scenario was the last synaptic firings of a guilty and dying chemo-infused brain.

But no, James concluded, that was not it at all. He was not dying. He had already died. He was dead. And now he was resurrected with a racist, murderous Louisiana marshall sitting above him, attempting to wait out his prey.

James had always been liked. As a

child, his mother had been busy and their life solitary. So he had not received much love or attention. So from his birth, James had honed the skill of being charming, helpful, and likable. And so being liked became the air he breathed.

And now, as he listened to the marshall seated on the floor above him, he began to see how being liked had been perhaps his own personal idolatry. For now he was living—yes, very much alive!—in a world where most people would not know, trust, or even like him. *Is it a desire to be perfect in the eyes of others?* he asked himself. *I wish I weren't so me-minded.* He pondered the question continually as he sat there, cramped: How does one go about losing a desire to be liked? And hadn't it been his desire to be liked that had made him lose his soul by turning a blind eye?

James found a little metal chamber pot and held it close to his skin. He unzipped his pants and peed into it, letting the stream of urine fall against the pan's side soundlessly. It was good to pee normally again, without the use of a catheter. He slowly returned the pan to the dirt floor, then stared out into the darkness, his eyes already accommodated to the black cellar. Remnants from previous cellmates surrounded him: several cups, a cast-off shoe, a bloody and torn shirt. Former escaped slaves. Had they all escaped safely? James wondered. Would he himself escape? Would God resurrect him and transport him in time only to have him murdered? James decided that that probably wasn't likely. That's not the God I know. He's neither so petty nor so slick. That's more like what one of the godfathers would do.

Marshall Albert stayed in the house till break of day, and only left the next morning when his posse returned to say the Black priest had not been found.

But even after James heard the relieved, "God be with you, Marshall," and the defeated, angry closing of the door, the Brackners did not open the door of James' little cell. So James sat there, crouched, cramped, waiting. All morning, the family walked inside and out, doing chores, greeting several housewives who arrived from neighbouring homes. And still James was not freed. The trap door was opened, twice. Once to remove the chamber pot. Once to bring him honey baked ham with beans. Night came again, and he was not freed. "We know what we're doing," Jacob Brackner said.

So, for three nights and three days, James ate, shat, slept, and peed in that darkness. Then, at last, he was released.

Climbing up, he had to train his eyes to accept the light again.

"They're gone," Jacob said, helping James climb up. "Sorry for keeping you down there so long, Father. But it's safer this way. Couldn't close the shutters. And they'd be watching. Next week or two you stay in. Don't go running out or talk about how you got cabin fever. Even if they think you ain't here, they'll be roundabout, snooping."

"Got ya!" James said, and looked around the cabin.

He never set foot outside and steered clear of the windows. The exile seemed strange but familiar. In the hospital, he had endured a similar kind of prison. Not being able to go out. Being waited on and cared for, yet somehow at the mercy of and dependent on everyone around him.

"Is this the way it will always be in this new life of mine?" he asked God. "Will I always be remembering my death and the circumstances around it?"

Some three weeks later, he was told one morning that he would be leaving for free state territory that night. He would be leaving by night, by covered wagon, and Quakers in Kansas would help him found his school if that was what he wanted to do.

"Yes," he said, shaking Jacob's hand profusely, "that is what I want to do."

His only parting gift to his saviours was to tell them about the future war, about a president named Abraham Lincoln, and to suggest that perhaps they should move far away.

So, that night, after hugging the missus tightly and giving the young 'un a tight squeeze on his shoulder, Father James McLaren went on his way.

In Kansas, he would find many who did not like him. He did not seek their love. He would find prey and those who preyed upon them. He hooked up with the prey.

His attempts to create a rainbow school challenged even his benefactors. His school flourished, but he died deeply disliked. And as he lay in his little room, surrounded by orphans young and old, he was happy for it. His life had become a thing of beauty.

RAISING THE VEIL

By Zoey Xolton

Alana clutched her bouquet, her wedding dress billowing in the darkness. She stood patiently, waiting for her groom. Where was he? For that matter, where was everyone else? Something wasn't quite right. Her fingers were too thin, her gown—torn and stained. Panic rose inside her. She reached for her throat, to find that she didn't have one.

She was bones.

Then it came flooding back to her. The accident! She'd never walked down the aisle. *She was dead.* And one thing was for certain… She wasn't resting in peace. She was alone, and judging by her untended grave? Long forgotten.

First published in *Forest of Fear*, Blood Song Books, 2019

LOCKDOWN PHANTOM #1

ABOUT THE PUBLISHER

BLACK HARE PRESS is a small, independent publisher based in Melbourne, Australia.

Founded in 2018, our aim has always been to champion emerging authors from all around the globe and offer opportunities for them to participate in speculative fiction and horror short story anthologies.

Connect

Website: *www.blackharepress.com*

Twitter: *@BlackHarePress*

BLACK HARE PRESS

LOCKDOWN PHANTOM #1

LOCKDOWN PHANTOM #1

LOCKDOWN PHANTOM #1